Summer Trouble?

A whole crowd of people gathered around, pointing and laughing.

Stephanie looked up at what they were pointing at and shrieked. "My racing suit!"

Her bright orange swimsuit hung from the high diving board. Pinned to it was a big sign. Stephanie felt her cheeks burn as she read it:

> CLUB STEPHANIE, WATCH OUT!
> THE FLAMINGOES WILL BEAT THE
> BATHING SUITS OFF YOU!

The Flamingoes circled around Rene and Alyssa. They all laughed and slapped high fives. Rick stood next to them. He stared up at Stephanie's racing suit—and laughed, too!

Rick probably thinks I'm a total loser now, Stephanie thought. *Well, I'll show him—and the Flamingoes,* she vowed. *I'll show all of them!*

Club Stephanie will win this race, if it's the last thing we do!

Full House™: Stephanie novels

Phone Call from a Flamingo
The Boy-Oh-Boy Next Door
Twin Troubles
Hip Hop Till You Drop
Here Comes the Brand-New Me
The Secret's Out
Daddy's Not-So-Little Girl
P.S. Friends Forever
Getting Even with the Flamingoes
The Dude of My Dreams
Back-to-School Cool
Picture Me Famous
Two-for-One Christmas Fun
The Big Fix-up Mix-up
Ten Ways to Wreck a Date
Wish Upon a VCR
Doubles or Nothing
Sugar and Spice Advice
Never Trust a Flamingo
The Truth About Boys
Crazy About the Future

Club Stephanie:

#1 Fun, Sun, and Flamingoes
#2 Fireworks and Flamingoes

Available from MINSTREL Books

FULL HOUSE™
Club Stephanie

Fireworks and Flamingoes

**Based on the hit Warner Bros.
TV series**

Emily Ecco

A Parachute Press Book

READING

A MINSTREL®
BOOK

Published by POCKET BOOKS
New York   London   Toronto   Sydney   Tokyo   Singapore

This book is a work of fiction. Names, characters, places and incidents are products of the author's imagination or are used fictitiously. Any resemblance to actual events or locales or persons, living or dead, is entirely coincidental.

A MINSTREL PAPERBACK *Original*

 A Minstrel Book published by
POCKET BOOKS, a division of Simon & Schuster Inc.
1230 Avenue of the Americas, New York, NY 10020

A PARACHUTE PRESS BOOK

 Copyright © and ™ 1997 by Warner Bros.

FULL HOUSE, characters, names and all related indicia are trademarks of Warner Bros. © 1997.

All rights reserved, including the right to reproduce this book or portions thereof in any form whatsoever. For information address Pocket Books, 1230 Avenue of the Americas, New York, NY 10020

ISBN: 0-671-00827-7

First Minstrel Books printing July 1997

10 9 8 7 6 5 4 3

A MINSTREL BOOK and colophon are registered trademarks of Simon & Schuster Inc.

Cover photo by Schultz Photography

Printed in the U.S.A.

CHAPTER

1

◆ ◂ ◖ ◆

Stephanie Tanner stood behind the bushes by the picnic tables and peered through the dark. *I can't believe I'm seeing this! I can't believe it!* she thought.

She quickly turned away. She couldn't bear to watch Rick, her new boyfriend, kiss Rene—her worst enemy.

"Oh, no. Oh, Steph! You were right," blurted Darcy Powell, Stephanie's best friend. "Coming here was a really, really, bad idea."

Stephanie swiped blindly at the tears that suddenly filled her eyes. "How could he do this to me? I can't believe it," she said. "I trusted him!"

"I'm sorry, Steph," Darcy murmured.

Stephanie squared her shoulders. "No—I can't

let this happen," she declared. "I *won't* let Rene ruin everything between Rick and me! I won't!"

"Face it, Steph," Darcy said. "Rene just stole your boyfriend. What can you do?"

"I don't know," Stephanie told her. "But this isn't the end, Darcy. I'm going to do something. And when I do, Rene better watch out!"

"Okay, I'm stumped," Stephanie admitted later that night. "I can't think of the right way to get back at Rene. I can't be as nasty and sneaky as the Flamingoes. That would make me just as bad as they are."

Stephanie and her friends were back at Kayla Norris's house for their Friday night sleepover.

"I hate those Flamingoes!" said Darcy Powell, Stephanie's best friend. She shook her head so hard that her black hair swung against her cheek.

The Flamingoes were a super-snobby group of girls. They always hung out together, wearing the latest outfits in their favorite color, bright pink. And they were always mean to Stephanie and her friends.

"Why do they have to ruin *everything*?" Stephanie complained. "Just once, I'd like to get even with them!"

"Me too," agreed Allie Taylor, Stephanie's other best friend.

Allie was usually quiet and kind of shy. Darcy was athletic and full of energy. But both Allie and Darcy agreed that the Flamingoes were bad news.

"Going after the guys we like is their meanest trick ever!" Allie scowled. "I wish I never thought of spying on the picnic tonight."

Allie had been worried about her friend Chad and Flamingo Alyssa Norman going to the lifeguard picnic together.

"At least Chad only put his arm around Alyssa," Stephanie pointed out. "Rick was *kissing* Rene!"

"Well, I'm not getting upset about Chad anymore," Allie declared. "He's history."

"What do you mean?" Stephanie asked.

"I mean, I thought I liked him. And I thought he liked me," Allie replied. "But we only went on one date. And if he's going to flirt with other girls the minute I'm not around, then I don't want him anymore."

"Good for you! You're better off without him," Kayla agreed.

Kayla was new to their group of friends. She had met Darcy the year before when they both swam for the San Francisco City swim team. She met the others just over a week ago, at the community center pool where they were camp counselors. She quickly became a good friend.

"My mom always says, another guy will come

along any minute," Kayla went on. "Just forget all about Chad."

"Chad? Who's Chad?" Allie pretended to think hard.

Anna Rice burst out laughing. "Good one, Allie!" She clapped Allie on the back, making her stack of bangle bracelets jingle noisily.

Anna was also a new friend. She was outgoing and full of enthusiasm, and had her own unique sense of style. She loved making her own clothes and buying things in thrift shops, and putting them together in unusual combinations—like the ankle-length black silk skirt and cropped blue sweatshirt she wore today. Anna turned to Stephanie with a wide smile spread across her freckled face.

"Stephanie?" Anna questioned. "You're not laughing."

Stephanie sighed. "Sorry," she murmured. "I wish I could laugh. I wish I could forget about Rick. But . . ."

"Hold it right there," Kayla told her. "Rick is a total creep. We all saw him kissing Rene! Don't even *think* about thinking about him!"

"I know you're right, Kayla," Stephanie began. "But I can't help it. Maybe there's some reason why Rick kissed Rene. Something I don't know about."

Darcy looked at her as if she were crazy. "What kind of reason could there be?"

"I don't know," Stephanie admitted.

"Well, it won't do you any good to think about Rick," Darcy said. "Kayla is right—that's over."

"Right. You shouldn't think about him, talk to him, see him—" Kayla began.

"Oh, no!" Stephanie exclaimed.

"What is it?" Kayla asked.

"How can I *not* see him? Rick and Rene will be together at the pool every day!" Stephanie groaned. "How will I live through it?"

Rick, Rene, Alyssa, and Chad were all assistant lifeguards at the community center pool—the same pool where Stephanie and her friends ran their day camp for little kids, Club Stephanie.

Rene and the rest of the Flamingoes hung out together under a big pink umbrella, acting as if they ran the place. It was impossible to ignore them.

"Poor Steph." Allie said. "How *will* you get through the summer?"

"I won't," Stephanie declared. "I can't go back to the pool, ever again."

"But you have to," Anna pointed out. "You can't drop out of camp. The whole Club Stephanie day camp was your idea."

"And you can't let Rene and the Flamingoes win, either," Darcy added. "If you stay away from the pool, Rene will be more impossible than ever!"

"Right. You have to act like she doesn't bother you at all," Kayla put in.

"Okay, okay!" Stephanie exclaimed. "I know you're all right. I'll go—but it won't be easy. Rene said she'd get Rick. And she did! She'll be gloating and bragging. . . . Oh, she just makes me so mad!"

And what about Rick . . . ? Stephanie wondered. But she couldn't think about Rick. She had liked him so much! She'd spent hours dreaming of the perfect summer they were going to have together. Now she could only picture him with Rene.

"I have an idea!" Darcy sat up straighter on the bed. "We'll go to the pool with you tomorrow, Steph. That way you can face Rene with all your friends around you."

"Tomorrow? So soon?" Stephanie swallowed over the lump that suddenly formed in her throat.

"I can't go tomorrow," Allie said. "I have to visit my aunt."

"And I promised to help my mom with chores all day," Anna added.

Anna's family had only recently moved to San Francisco. They were still busy getting their house unpacked.

"That's okay," Stephanie said with relief. "I'd

rather go on Sunday. The pool is less crowded then, and maybe there won't be so many Flamingoes around."

"Sounds good to me," Kayla said. The others quickly agreed.

"Then it's settled," Stephanie said. "We hit the pool Sunday, together. Thanks, you guys. I feel tons better already."

"Enough about the Flamingoes. It's time to party!" Kayla punched on her CD player, and bouncy music filled her bedroom.

Stephanie smiled as her friends began dancing. She leaped to her feet and joined them.

I won't let Rene get to me, she told herself. *Not Rene, or any of the Flamingoes. This can still be my best summer ever!*

CHAPTER

2

◆ ◀ ◆ ◆

Stephanie quickly glanced around. "Great! The pool is practically deserted!" she exclaimed.

It was Sunday morning at the community center. There was no camp today and no other scheduled activities.

No kids swarmed over the playing fields, no crowd lined up in the snack shack, not a single person swam in the water. Pete, the senior lifeguard, watched over an empty pool.

Best of all, Rene wasn't there yet, and there were no other Flamingoes in sight.

"Thanks for coming with me, Allie," Stephanie said. "I'm still really nervous about seeing Rene today. And Rick, too. I couldn't even talk to him when he called."

"Rick called you?" Allie asked.

"Three times," Stephanie said.

Allie looked amazed. "Wow. Chad never called me. Not once. He dumped me for Alyssa, and that was it." Allie sighed heavily. She ducked her head so that her reddish brown hair fell over her face, hiding her green eyes.

"Really?" Stephanie felt badly for Allie, but she couldn't help feeling a small burst of hope for herself.

Maybe Rick still likes me, she thought. *Maybe he was calling to apologize for being with Rene! Maybe it was all a big mistake.*

"Hey, you guys! We're over here!" Darcy waved wildly from the entrance to the community center. Darcy looked great in her favorite shorts set. The light green outfit was especially pretty against Darcy's dark skin. And it showed off her strong, athletic figure.

Anna and Kayla hurried beside Darcy.

"Hey, guys!" Kayla smoothed down her long blond hair, then tucked her blue-and-white-checked shirt into her denim shorts.

"Cute outfit," Stephanie told her.

"Thanks," Kayla said. "It's new." She tried to hide a big yawn. "I can't believe we're here so early."

"It is early," Anna agreed. "I just threw on the first thing I could find this morning."

Stephanie tried not to grin. Today Anna had thrown on full red harem pants and a faded print shirt from a thrift shop.

"Oh, uh! It's not early enough!" Darcy nudged Stephanie. "Here come the Flamingoes!"

The Flamingoes paraded into the pool area, wearing matching pink bikinis: Tiffany Schroeder, Cynthia Hanson, Dominique Dobson, Darah Judson, and Tina Brewer. They grabbed pool chairs and pulled them into a circle, talking and laughing loudly.

A group of boys rushed into the pool area after them. They helped set up the Flamingoes' bright pink fringed umbrella.

"Here comes Alyssa Norman," Allie murmured. "And she's with Chad."

Stephanie looked up as Chad and Alyssa strolled into the pool area together. They both wore their red lifeguard outfits—a tank suit for Alyssa, swim shorts with a tank top for Chad.

Alyssa stopped to say hello to her Flamingo friends. She pulled her ash blond hair into a high ponytail, then adjusted her white baseball cap over it. She hurried to sit on the lifeguard chair next to Chad. He wrapped an arm around her shoulders and gave her a hug. Then he bent down and kissed the tip of her nose.

Allie's cheeks went pale, but she tossed back her head. "They don't bother me one bit. Let's change into our suits and hit the pool."

"Sounds good to me," Stephanie told her as they headed into the locker room.

"Hey, wait, you guys! Check out this notice!" Darcy pointed to a poster pinned to the bulletin board outside the locker room. "The community center is having a big Fourth of July celebration."

Stephanie read through the notice quickly. "Games with prizes, peewee races for the little kids, a picnic, and fireworks at night! I love fireworks!"

"That's not the best part," Darcy said. "Look at the list of races. There's a swimming medley listed."

"What's that?" Stephanie asked.

"It's a relay race for four swimmers," Darcy explained in growing excitement. "Each person swims a different stroke, like backstroke, butterfly, crawl, and freestyle. You have to finish two laps each, and the fastest team wins. It's a really fun race."

"Sounds like fun—for you and Kayla," Stephanie said. "You guys are great swimmers."

"And I never swim," Anna reminded them. "I hate swimming."

"Okay, so you won't swim," Darcy told Anna. "But the rest of us can. We could be the Club Stephanie relay team."

"I don't think so." Allie shook her head.

"Oh, come on! You, me, Kayla, and Stephanie— it would be a blast! After all, it's just for fun," Darcy said.

"But who would we swim against?" Stephanie asked.

"Not the Flamingoes, I hope." Allie shivered. "They're incredible swimmers."

"Allie's right," Anna said. "Alyssa and Rene are super-fast. And Julie Chu is practically a backstroking goddess."

"They'd clobber us in a race," Stephanie agreed. "And the last thing we need right now is to lose anything to the Flamingoes!"

"Shhh," Darcy warned. "Here come Rene and Mary."

Stephanie whirled around as Rene and Mary Kelly stepped through the entrance to the community center and headed toward the clubhouse.

Rene tossed her blond hair back over one shoulder. She straightened the waist of the crisp white shorts she had pulled over her red lifeguard suit.

"Rene sure loves that lifeguard outfit," Kayla murmured. "She wears it constantly."

"She'd probably wear it to the mall if she could," Anna jooked.

Stephanie burst out laughing.

"Shhh!" Anna warned. "Here she comes!"

"What's so funny?" Rene demanded. She stopped by the bulletin board and stared at Stephanie.

"Yeah, what are you smiling about?" Mary demanded. She reached to tighten the pink scarf that held her black hair in place. The scarf matched her ultra-tight pink racing suit. Stephanie had never seen the suit before.

"Oh, hi, Rene. Hi, Mary," Stephanie said in a casual tone. "I didn't see you there."

"Yeah, right." Mary snorted. "As if you didn't notice my new suit right away. Pretty cool, huh?"

Anna shrugged. "If you want to look like a pink sausage."

Stephanie giggled.

"I'm surprised you feel like laughing at anything, Stephanie," Rene told her. "But then, I guess you don't know about me and Rick yet."

"Rick *really* likes Rene," Mary added with a smirk.

"He's so cool," Rene said dreamily. "And a great kisser, you know."

"How would she know that?" Mary teased.

"Oh, I forgot!" Rene exclaimed. "Rick wasn't

kissing *you*, he was kissing *me*. At the lifeguards' cookout." She tossed her head again. "It's really too bad you weren't there Friday night," she went on. "But don't say I didn't warn you. I told you I could steal Rick away from you."

"Poor, poor Stephanie." Mary shook her head and sighed, pretending to feel sorry for her.

Stephanie felt her cheeks burning with anger. *I will not let them get to me*, she told herself.

She lifted her chin and stared Rene right in the eyes. "As if I cared about Rick! I wasn't really interested in him, anyway," she lied.

"Oh, really?" Rene gave her a scornful glance. "Sorry if I don't believe you."

"Believe it," Stephanie said. "Anyway, Rene, we were talking about something important—before you interrupted." Stephanie turned her back on Rene and Mary and studied the bulletin board.

Rene stepped up to the poster. "What's all this about the Fourth of July?"

"Don't bother reading it, Rene," Darcy told her. "You wouldn't be interested."

"I'll decide that." She read the notice. "Hey, this sounds cool," she told Mary. "We could form a team for the swimming races."

"Who would we race around here?" Mary pointed to Stephanie and her friends. "We've seen *them* swim. And they stink!"

"You're wrong, Mary," Rene said in a fake sweet voice. "They could win a race—against their Club Stephanie campers!"

Mary hooted with laughter. "Don't worry, Stephanie. We won't compete against you guys. We don't want to slaughter you in public."

"Oh, yeah?" Stephanie said. "We could destroy you in the medley relay—if we wanted to."

"Uh, hold on, Steph!" Allie poked Stephanie hard in the side and gave her a look of alarm. Anna was staring at Stephanie as if she were crazy. Even Kayla looked uneasy.

"Is that a challenge?" Rene demanded.

"Sure," Stephanie said.

"Okay, you're on." Rene nodded. "The Flamingoes against Club Stephanie."

"It'll be a blast, beating you wimps," Mary added.

"Let's make it even more fun," Stephanie replied. "How about a real bet? If you lose, you can't wear anything pink for one day!"

Mary's mouth dropped open.

"No, wait—" Stephanie added. "You *can* wear pink." She grinned. "Pink shower caps!"

"You don't scare us," Rene said. "It's a deal. The losing team wears shower caps to the pool—for one whole day!"

"No problem." Stephanie held her hand out to

15

Rene. "Let's shake on it. Unless you're too chicken?"

Rene shook her hand. "See you in your shower caps, losers!" She smirked at Stephanie one last time, then she and Mary hurried away.

Stephanie watched them go. There was a moment of silence.

"Uh, Steph," Allie finally asked, "didn't you get a little carried away? I mean, what if we lose?"

Stephanie suddenly imagined herself walking past Rick, pretending she didn't care what he thought of her—while she was wearing a shower cap!

She cringed.

Oh, no, she thought. *What if we don't win? What have I done now?*

CHAPTER
3

$\blacklozenge$ $\blacktriangleleft$ $\blacklozenge$ $\blacklozenge$

"Steph, I don't believe you did that!" Allie groaned. "We're doomed!"

"I'm sorry, you guys," Stephanie answered. "It just kind of happened."

"That's for sure! I mean, I know how you felt," Allie told her. "Rene makes me mad, too. But we'll never beat the Flamingoes. We're going to lose that race in front of *everyone!*"

"Hey, the Flamingoes aren't *that* great," Darcy argued. "I'm as good as Alyssa or Rene. And you've never seen Kayla's backstroke. She could beat Julie without breaking a sweat."

"Sure. But what about Allie and me? We're just average swimmers," Stephanie pointed out.

"Hold on," Kayla told her. "Darcy and I can coach you."

"Sure—I was going to help you with your swimming this summer, anyway, remember?" Darcy added. "And there's still two weeks till the picnic. That's enough time, if we work hard."

"Do you really mean that, Darce?" Stephanie asked. "Or are you just trying to make me feel better? Because none of us will feel better if we work hard, and then we still lose."

"No, I really mean it," Darcy insisted. "I even have a plan for the race. Kayla and I are the best swimmers, so we'll swim first, to give our team a strong lead. Then you and Allie won't have to swim as fast as we do."

"That's a great strategy," Kayla agreed. "I think we really have a chance at winning."

"If you both say so, I guess I believe it," Allie said.

"Winning would be great," Stephanie admitted.

"Great!" Darcy beamed. "We'll work hard and beat those Flamingoes by a mile—in front of everyone!"

"Listen, you guys." Kayla glanced around uneasily. "Maybe we should get out of here and go someplace where we can *really* talk strategy—without any Flamingoes around."

"Good idea," Stephanie agreed. "Besides, I don't

much feel like hanging around the pool right now."

"Let's hit that new ice cream store at the mall!" Kayla suggested.

"Isn't it too early for ice cream?" Allie asked.

"Is it ever too early?" Darcy joked. "I'm with Kayla. Let's go!"

Twenty minutes later, they were seated in the food court at the mall with huge ice cream sundaes in front of them. Anna sipped at a glass of water.

"Are you sure you don't want anything else?" Stephanie asked Anna.

"I'm sure," she said. "I'm trying to cut down on sweets."

Stephanie dug into her sundae. "Good for you," she said. "I can never resist the hot fudge special." She took another taste.

"Okay, let's get down to business," Darcy said. "First, we'll work out our swimming order."

"You know, I should call my cousin Cody to-night," Kayla said. "He's our age, and he's a fan-tastic swimmer. He helped coach his school team, and they won first place in the state last year."

"Really? Do you think he'd give us some pointers?" Stephanie asked.

"Sure," Kayla said. "I call him for advice all the time. And I know the first thing he'd say—we need a strict training schedule. We—"

"Uh-oh. Don't look now," Darcy interrupted in a low voice. "But you won't believe who just walked in."

Stephanie glanced up and froze.

Rick was crossing the food court. His little brother, Austin, was with him. And they were heading right toward her!

Rick raised a hand to push his blond bangs away from his blue eyes. Stephanie felt her heart lurch. He was so cute!

Stephanie quickly dropped her gaze. Her heart began to pound. Was Rick coming over to talk to her? Did he want to explain about the cookout—and the kiss?

Maybe he wants to apologize, she thought. *Maybe we could still get back together again!*

"Remember, Stephanie, don't talk to him," Kayla warned. "Not one word."

"Right. Just think about what he did to you," Anna added. "You don't need a guy who likes Rene."

"Uh, right," Stephanie mumbled.

"Rick, look!" Austin shrieked. "There's Stephanie, from camp! She let me play battle tag!" Austin broke away from Rick and ran up to the table. "Hey, Stephanie! What are you doing here?"

Stephanie forced a smile. "Hey, Austin. My friends and I are just having some ice cream."

Austin glanced up at Rick. "Don't you want to say hi to Stephanie?" he asked.

Rick scowled. "Not really," he replied. "I mean, she won't talk to me on the phone. So why should I talk to her?"

"I—" Stephanie started to say. Kayla kicked Stephanie's ankle under the table.

"Rickie, I want an ice cream," Austin said. "A big one!"

Rick looked at Austin, then at Stephanie. "Maybe one of Stephanie's friends will help you," he said.

Stephanie glanced at Rick in surprise. "Why should they do that?"

"Because we need to talk," Rick replied.

"I'll take Austin." Anna leaped up. She grabbed Austin's hand and led him to the ice cream counter.

Rick stared at Stephanie. "Well?" he asked.

Stephanie felt Kayla, Darcy, and Allie watching her. "Well, what?" she replied. "You're the one who wants to talk. I don't know what we have to talk about!"

"Good answer," Kayla murmured.

"What is going on, Stephanie?" Rick demanded. "We were supposed to go on another date. The next thing I know, you're not talking to me. What do you think you're doing?"

"What am *I* doing? That's a laugh," Stephanie mumbled.

"I don't get it. Why are you acting this way?" Rick asked.

"As if you don't know," she retorted.

"Well, I don't," Rick insisted.

"Okay, I'll spell it out for you," Stephanie told him. *"R-e-n-e."*

"Huh? What are you talking about?" Rick asked.

Allie exchanged a look of surprise with Stephanie. "I'll tell you what she's talking about—Friday night," Allie blurted. "The cookout? You and Rene? The way you kissed her. Remember now?"

"The way I *what?*" Rick looked astonished. Then a grin slowly spread across his face. "Oh, that!" He chuckled.

"It's nothing to laugh about," Stephanie snapped, feeling a burst of anger.

"Hold on," Rick told her. "I can explain what happened."

"Oh, I saw what happened," Stephanie said. "We all did!"

Rick stared at her. "What do you mean, you all saw?" he asked. "You weren't even there!"

Stephanie flushed. "We weren't supposed to be there," she admitted.

"We were driving by, and we happened to stop

at the pool to, uh, look for something," Kayla told him.

Rick narrowed his eyes. "You spied on me?" he asked Stephanie. "With all your friends?"

"Good thing, too," Kayla declared. "Or else Steph and Allie would never have known what rats you guys really are."

"I can't believe it," Rick said to Stephanie. "I can't believe you spied on me! I would never do that to you."

"You wouldn't have to!" Stephanie said, louder than she intended. "I wouldn't go around kissing anyone else."

Rick glanced across the table at Allie, Darcy, and Kayla. His jaw clenched. He turned angrily to Stephanie again. "I guess I'm lucky that I found out what you're really like."

"Hold on," Stephanie cried. "I'm the one who's mad at you!"

"Not anymore," Rick replied in a tight voice. He spun on his heel and marched over to the ice cream counter. He grabbed Austin by the hand. "Let's go," Stephanie heard him say.

"But can't we talk to Stephanie some more?" Austin asked.

"No. I only talk to *friends*," Rick answered. He pulled Austin across the food court, and he didn't look back.

Stephanie swallowed hard. How had everything gotten all turned around? *Rick is the one who did the wrong thing—not me,* she told herself.

She blinked her eyes quickly a few times, trying not to cry. She saw Darcy and Allie exchange a sympathetic look.

"Remember, Stephanie, don't let him bother you," Kayla advised. "Forget about Rick. You don't want someone who likes Rene, anyway. Do you?"

"I guess not."

"You guess not?" Kayla questioned.

"I mean, I don't know why I ever cared about Rick at all," Stephanie declared.

"That's better," Kayla said.

"Good for you, Steph," Darcy added.

Yeah, good for me, Stephanie thought. *The only trouble is, I'm lying!*

CHAPTER

4

◆ ◀ ◆ ◆

"Please pass the orange juice," Stephanie said. It was the next morning, and her family was gathered around the kitchen table.

Michelle picked up the oversize carton. "Overhand or underhand?" she asked. She held the carton as if it were a football.

"I guess that's a nine-year-old's idea of a joke." Stephanie sighed. "Just give me the juice, Michelle."

Michelle grinned and handed the juice to her eighteen-year-old sister, D.J. D.J. was dressed in a crisp blue suit. She was working at her first summer job in an office downtown.

D.J. thought having a real job was very grown-up. But Stephanie also knew that D.J. was a little jealous of Stephanie's job at the pool. After all, Stephanie could go to work in a bathing suit, while D.J. had to work in a business suit!

D.J. carefully poured the juice so she wouldn't spill any on her clean outfit. Then she handed the carton to Stephanie.

"Finally!" Stephanie said as she poured her own glass.

"That's one of the problems with living in such a big family," Joey Gladstone said. "It takes so long to get your food!" Joey had lived with the family for years, helping Danny raise Stephanie, D.J., and Michelle after their mother died.

Stephanie's uncle Jesse plopped two brown paper bags down in front of Alex and Nicky, his twin four-year-old boys. Jesse and the boys lived in the attic apartment along with Stephanie's aunt Becky.

Becky was already at work. She and Stephanie's dad, Danny Tanner, were co-hosts of *Good Morning, San Francisco*, a public television program. Danny was going to the station later that morning. For now, he bent over the stove, helping himself to a second cup of coffee.

"Peanut butter and fluff," Jesse told the boys. "The favorite lunch of kids everywhere! Now you guys can picnic in style."

"Yummy!" Alex said.

"Hey, that reminds me of something important," Stephanie said. "Sandy is planning a special Fourth of July picnic for the whole community center. Families are invited. And the Club Stephanie counselors are entering a swimming relay race."

"That's neat, Steph," Danny told her. "You know how pleased I am that you girls are working on your swimming this summer."

"And this afternoon is our first real swim practice," Stephanie told him. "So I might be late for dinner."

"That's okay. Just call later and let me know," Danny said.

"Will there be fireworks at the picnic?" D.J. asked.

"Yup. As soon as it gets dark," Stephanie replied.

"I love fireworks!" Michelle exclaimed.

"Fireworks! Fireworks!" Alex chanted.

"Big boom!" Nicky yelled.

Jesse chuckled. "Sorry, you guys," he said. "But that will be way past your bedtime. We can have pretend fireworks at home."

"Well, I'm thinking of bringing a date for the fireworks," D.J. said. "They're so romantic!" She sighed dreamily. "What about you, Steph?" she asked. "Will you have a date that night with Rick?"

27

Stephanie tried not to show how upset she was at the mention of Rick's name. "Uh, probably not," she said. She glanced at her watch. "Yikes—I'm late for camp. See you all later!" She grabbed her backpack and ran out the door.

Stephanie barely made it to camp on time. She threw her backpack into her locker without even stopping to change into her bathing suit. She raced to the picnic area where they held Club Stephanie. The tables were crowded. There must have been more than twenty campers—more than they'd ever had before!

Anna, Darcy, Allie, and Kayla were running from table to table, handing out art supplies. Stephanie rushed up to them. "What's going on? Where did all these campers come from?"

"The Flamingoes closed their camp," Anna told her.

"Sandy was waiting to tell us when we got here this morning," Darcy added. "All the Little Flamingoes are going to Club Stephanie now!"

"You're kidding!" Stephanie's mouth dropped open in astonishment. "Sandy told you that?"

Sandy Kovacs was the activities director at the community center. She was the one who first asked Stephanie to begin a day camp. Sandy thought there was a real need for a camp at the pool. Then the Flamingoes decided to start a camp, too—the Little Flamingoes.

"I guess taking care of little kids was too hard for the Flamingoes." Stephanie laughed. "But this makes Club Stephanie a real success!"

Stephanie pitched in to help with the art project. The morning flew past. Soon it was time for the campers to have their swimming lesson.

"I need to change into my bathing suit," Stephanie told Allie and the others. "I'll meet you guys at the pool."

She raced to the locker room in the clubhouse. Her locker door was already open.

Oops, guess I forgot to lock it this morning, she thought.

She reached inside her locker for her backpack and dug through it, searching for her bright orange racing suit.

That's funny. I know I put my suit in here last night.

Stephanie frowned. She turned over her backpack and spilled everything out. Towel. Goggles. Sunglasses. Sunscreen. Lip balm. A novel called *Summer Love* that she hadn't finished yet. Keys. A list of the Club Stephanie campers' home phone numbers. Silver toenail polish. And one piece of dusty gum.

But no racing suit.

"Okay, okay, so I guess I *didn't* put it in here,"

she mumbled. She tossed everything back into her backpack. *I'll just have to borrow an extra suit from someone,* she told herself.

She hurried back outside and headed toward the pool. A whole crowd of people gathered around, pointing and laughing.

Stephanie looked up at what they were pointing at and shrieked. "So that's what happened to my racing suit!"

Her bright orange suit hung from the high diving board—and pinned to it was a big sign. Stephanie felt her cheeks burn as she read it:

CLUB STEPHANIE, WATCH OUT!
THE FLAMINGOES WILL BEAT THE BATHING SUITS OFF YOU!

The Flamingoes circled around Rene and Alyssa. They all laughed and slapped high fives. Rick stood next to them. He stared up at Stephanie's racing suit—and laughed, too!

"They're not getting away with this!" Stephanie fumed.

She pushed through the crowd, making her way over to the high dive. She raced up the ladder, walked out onto the diving board, and yanked her suit off the end. The crowd burst into applause.

Stephanie felt her cheeks flaming bright red. She

had never been so embarrassed! She climbed down the ladder as fast as she could and pulled the sign off her suit. Furiously she crushed it into a ball. The crowd started to drift away.

"Oh, Steph! I can't believe they did this to you!" Darcy hurried up to Stephanie.

"I know!" Stephanie stared down at her suit. "How can I ever wear this again?" she asked. "Everyone will laugh when they see it."

"Don't worry. You can borrow my extra suit for today," Darcy told her. "It's black."

Stephanie sighed. "Thanks, but on second thought, I'd better not. That will only make the Flamingoes think they really got to me. I'll have to wear my suit and pretend I don't mind."

Stephanie hurried into the locker room to change.

Rick probably thinks I'm a total loser now, she thought. *Well, I'll show him—and the Flamingoes,* she vowed. *I'll show all of them!*

Club Stephanie will win this race if it's the last thing we do!

CHAPTER
5

◆ ◀ ▪ ◆

"Nice suit," Rene called as Stephanie made her way through the crowd around the pool.

Stephanie raised her head and walked past, ignoring Rene. The Club Stephanie campers were done with their swimming lesson. Now they splashed each other in the shallow end of the pool.

"Stephanie, watch me! You're not watching!" Austin yelled.

"Sorry, Austin!" Stephanie called back. She waded to the edge of the pool and leaned against the tiles. Kayla, Allie, and Darcy were in the water, splashing along with their campers.

"See what I can do?" Austin put his face in the water and blew bubbles.

"That's great!" Stephanie smiled. She had worried that it might be hard for her to take care of Austin, since she was so upset with Rick. But to her surprise, taking care of Rick's little brother didn't really bother her. Austin was a great kid. Plus, looking after Austin didn't make her think more about Rick—because she was already thinking about him constantly.

A bunch of other campers stuck their heads in the water, too. Tyler, Kelly, Trisha, and Jennifer blew bubbles, then stared at Stephanie.

"That was terrific," she told them. The kids all cheered.

"Hey, you guys—I just had the best idea for the picnic!" Anna appeared, wearing a bright, embroidered green vest over a white T-shirt. The vest looked great with her white cutoff jeans. "All the kids can make their own special flag and carry it in the Fourth of July parade. What do you think?"

"Sounds terrific," Stephanie told her.

"I want to make a flag now!" Brittany jumped up and ran over to Anna.

"Hold on." Anna laughed. "We can't have arts and crafts until your pool time is over."

"Do we *have* to have arts and crafts?" Tyler made a face. "Swimming is more fun. You should learn how to swim, Anna."

"Oh, I know how to swim," Anna told him. "I

33

just don't like it that much. You know me. I'm more into making things, like making lanyard necklaces and jewelry and stuff."

Club Stephanie had arts and crafts once each day, usually before swimming.

"You're so creative," Stephanie told her. "Did you make that vest you're wearing?"

"This? No way." Anna proudly stroked the pretty green vest. "My aunt sent this in the mail as an early birthday present."

"Your birthday!" Stephanie exclaimed. "When is it?"

"Sunday," Anna replied.

"Why didn't you tell us about it sooner?" Darcy demanded.

"It's no big deal." Anna shrugged. "I mean, I don't want to make a fuss about it."

"But we want to," Darcy declared.

"Yeah. You should at least have a party!" Allie exclaimed.

"A party?" Anna made a face. "I can't. You know we just moved here. My house is a total mess."

"I know what that's like," Allie said. "We redid our family room last year, and we had to pack up all our stuff into cartons. My mom said it was just like moving—total chaos."

"That's exactly it," Anna agreed. "Everything is

34

in boxes all over the place. Nothing is fixed up yet."

"Yeah. Decorating takes ages, doesn't it?" Allie asked. "It took forever for my mom and the decorator to decide what color scheme to use. And then it took twice as long for the new furniture to be delivered. Not to mention the new curtains, and the lamps and rugs! So I know what you're going through."

"Oh. Right. You said it," Anna mumbled.

"Anyway, I'm sure your house will look great, when you're done unpacking, I mean," Kayla added. "Right?"

"Oh, when we're done unpacking, it will practically be a palace!" Anna laughed.

"You know, I'm not sure where you live," Stephanie said. "Where is your house, anyway?"

"It's just over on Pacific Street," Anna replied. "One of those pink stucco houses."

"Pacific Street?" Allie asked. "Does your house have wrought-iron railings across the front?"

Anna hesitated. "Well, yeah, it does," she said.

"I know that house! It's practically a mansion!" Allie exclaimed. "Oh, Anna, you're so lucky! I always wished I could live there." She giggled. "I have this fantasy where my bedroom is on the second floor—one of those rooms with the fancy French doors and its own balcony."

"Wow. That sounds fantastic." Kayla gazed at Anna. "Does your room have its own balcony?"

"No way." Anna shook her head. "It has those railings, but my house isn't—"

"Though I'd choose a room with a view of the San Francisco Bay," Kayla interrupted. "That's *my* fantasy."

"I can't wait to see this house!" Stephanie cried.

"Yeah. As soon as you're ready, you'll have to have a huge party," Darcy added.

"But . . . I . . . it's not really—" Anna stammered.

"But we can't wait till then to have a party," Darcy cut in. "Anna's birthday is Sunday. So let's have her party somewhere else."

"Sure. We could have it at my house," Allie offered. "I love giving parties in our family room. What do you say, Anna?"

"Oh, well, I guess so. If you don't mind," Anna said.

"I don't mind!" Allie smiled. "It will be fun! I'll make us a special cake, too. What kind do you like best? Chocolate or yellow? Or carrot cake! I just found a *great* carrot cake recipe!"

"Oh, no," Stephanie groaned.

"Don't get Allie started on her favorite recipes," Darcy said. "You won't be able to get her to *stop* talking about them!"

Allie ignored them. "Do you like carrot cake, Anna?"

"I love it!" Anna's eyes lit up.

"Then it's settled," Allie said. "How about Saturday?"

"Great idea!" Kayla said. "We can wear our charm bracelets to make it our second official Club Stephanie sleepover."

Kayla had given everyone a bracelet with their name engraved on a delicate gold charm at their first sleepover.

"Me too," Stephanie said. "It will be loads of fun."

Anna smiled. "Thanks, you guys. I have to go home now. Let's talk more at camp tomorrow. The party sounds terrific."

A loud peal of laughter suddenly rang out. Stephanie saw Rene, Alyssa, Mary, and Julie Chu strutting toward the pool. They all wore pink racing suits and expensive swim goggles.

"They look like a professional swim team," Allie whispered.

Stephanie frowned. "That's not what worries me," she whispered back. "What worries me is that Baxter Davies is with them. And I'd like to know why!"

Baxter was nineteen and in college. He swam for his college swim team, and he was practically famous at the pool. He swam hundreds of practice laps every afternoon. Crawl, backstroke, breaststroke—he could swim them all, and *fast*.

"Hey, what's going on?" Darcy called to Rene. "What's Baxter doing with you guys?"

Rene grinned. "He's just doing what any swim coach would do."

Stephanie nearly choked. "Swim coach?" She exchanged a look of horror with her friends.

"That's right," Rene answered. "Baxter is our new trainer."

CHAPTER
6

♦ ◄ ◗ ♦

"Trainer? They talked Baxter into being their personal trainer?" Stephanie stared in disbelief as the Flamingoes headed for the deep end of the pool and gathered around Baxter.

"Okay, let's see what you can do," he told them. "Swim freestyle, two laps each. Julie first, then Rene, Alyssa, and Mary." Baxter lifted a clipboard and scribbled some notes.

The Flamingoes pulled on their goggles and swim caps. Julie stepped up to the lap lane that was roped off for serious swimmers. She squatted into a diving position.

"Take your mark—go!" Baxter clicked his stopwatch.

Julie dove. She sliced through the water at incredible speed. Baxter called out tips as she swam. She finished her lap, and Rene dove in.

"Rene is as fast as Julie—and Julie was incredible!" Allie gaped. "We might as well quit now."

"Don't say that," Darcy told her. "We'll, uh, just have to train a little harder than we thought."

"Yeah, we can still try our best," Kayla agreed.

"You'll see—I bet our practice goes great," Stephanie said. "Then just wait till those Flamingoes see what *we* can do!"

Camp ended. They ate lunch and had swim team practice.

But their practice didn't go great. They spent a lot of time deciding who would swim which stroke in the relay: Darcy would swim the butterfly, Kayla would do the backstroke. Allie chose freestyle, and Stephanie would swim the breaststroke.

Finally they tried a few practice relays, and their timing was terrible.

"Let's quit for today," Darcy said.

"Quit? But we didn't have much of a practice," Stephanie noted.

"It was only our first session," Kayla pointed out. "It's always slow to get a new team started."

"Sure. It'll go a lot better tomorrow," Darcy promised.

"Okay. If you're sure," Stephanie agreed.

They changed quickly into their clothes and headed home. Kayla took off toward her house. Stephanie, Allie, and Darcy biked in the opposite direction. As usual, Darcy turned off at her street and Stephanie and Allie continued on together.

"I know you think that was an easy practice, Steph," Allie began. "But I'm completely zonked." She steered her bike around the corner. "My arms feel like soggy spaghetti."

"Yeah, I'm starting to feel it, too," Stephanie agreed.

"Let's take a shortcut," Allie said. "I think we can go through on Grove Road if we turn left up ahead."

"I'm for that!" Stephanie followed Allie around the corner. "Hey—there's Anna!" she suddenly exclaimed.

Anna was several blocks ahead. It wasn't hard to recognize her beat-up mountain bike. Anna had painted it in zebra stripes with bright red handlebars.

"Hey! Anna! Anna, wait up!" Stephanie yelled. Anna was too far away to hear.

"Should we try to catch up?" Stephanie asked.

"Okay—if our legs hold out," Allie joked.

They pedaled harder. Up ahead, they saw Anna making a right-hand turn. They made the same turn a few minutes later and found themselves on Pacific Street.

"There's Anna's bike." Allie pointed to a very small, shabby pink stucco house. Anna's bike was locked up out front—but Anna must have already gone inside.

"That can't be her house," Stephanie said. She stared in surprise. The stucco was falling off in places. The tiny front porch sagged, and its rusty wrought-iron railing needed mending. The steps leading up to the porch were rotted away.

"You're right. Anna can't live *here*," Allie said. "She lives in that big pink mansion on the other end of the block."

"She could be visiting someone," Stephanie said.

"I guess so." Allie frowned. "But she's new in town, and she told us she doesn't have any other friends." Allie pointed at the rusty mailbox at the curb. "Besides, the mailbox has her name on it— Rice."

"But this doesn't make sense," Stephanie replied. "She told us she lived in a mansion. Why would she lie about it?"

"I guess we should ask her," Allie said. "Should I ring the bell or what?"

"Better not," Stephanie said quickly. "What if she thinks we were spying on her, the way I spied on Rick? I don't want Anna to get mad at us."

"You're right," Allie said. "I didn't even think about that! Now I feel kind of sneaky."

"Well, we didn't spy on purpose," Stephanie reminded her. "But let's get out of here before she finds out that we know where she really lives."

"That was awful, you guys!" Stephanie pulled off her swim goggles in disgust. "We're worse than yesterday! We have to do better than this!"

They were an hour into their afternoon practice.

"Don't worry, Steph, we'll get better," Darcy said. She glanced at her waterproof watch. "Let's try it again. The Flamingoes will be here for their practice in a few minutes."

"I wish we didn't have to share the lap lanes with them," Allie grumbled.

"I know. It's a drag." Stephanie glanced around the noisy pool. The afternoons were always crowded as the pool filled up with young kids and families. Only two lanes could be roped off for lap swimmers.

"We have both lanes to ourselves for now," Darcy said. "So let's not waste time."

"My cousin Cody suggested something to me last night on the phone," Anna said. "He said it sounded like Stephanie and Allie should keep their arms really close to their sides when they stroke."

"That could improve their form," Darcy agreed. "Let's try it."

"Okay." Stephanie pulled her goggles back on.

"Uh-oh—Flamingo alert," Kayla whispered. "They're early, too!"

Rene, Alyssa, Mary, and Julie appeared, trailing behind Baxter.

"Okay, guys, hit the water for a few warm-up laps," Baxter ordered. The Flamingoes got ready and dove into one of the lap lanes.

"I wish I knew why Baxter agreed to help them," Stephanie muttered.

"I heard that he's dating Mary's big sister, Erin," Allie told her. "I bet she talked him into it."

Stephanie stared as Julie stroked freestyle down the length of the pool. She hit the far wall and returned in no time.

"Looking good," Baxter called to her.

"She seems faster today than yesterday—and she's only warming up!" Stephanie groaned.

Allie shook her head in dismay. "They're going to kill us! They'll tear us to shreds and feed us to the sharks!"

"Don't freak out," Darcy said. "Baxter is good, but I think I'm a pretty good coach, too."

"You're great, Darcy, but face it—" Stephanie began. "You're no match for Baxter. You don't have his experience."

"Trainer or no trainer—we could still win this race," Darcy insisted. "Let's try a practice relay while the Flamingoes warm up. We'll pretend it's a real race and time ourselves."

Kayla leaped into the water. She put her feet up against the side of the pool. "Ready," she called.

Darcy held up her stopwatch. "Take your mark, go!" She clicked the stopwatch.

Kayla pushed off and streaked through the water.

"Hey, Julie!" Baxter called from the next lane. "Race that girl—let's see who's fastest."

"What! You can't start a race now. We're just practicing," Darcy protested. "Besides, Kayla already started."

"No problem. Julie can catch up." Baxter nodded to Julie, who stroked down her lane with incredible speed.

"Go, Julie!" the Flamingoes cheered.

Anna, Stephanie, Darcy, and Allie watched in amazement.

"What is she—part barracuda?" Darcy asked.

"Kayla is still way ahead," Allie said.

"Not by much," Stephanie replied. "And she started first!"

"Are we going to race them?" Allie asked.

"We're not going to let them beat us," Stephanie declared.

"Okay, then—I'm next," Darcy replied.

Kayla reached the end of the lane, tagged the wall, did an underwater somersault, and began swimming back.

Julie reached the end of her lane only seconds after Kayla. She did a smoother underwater somersault than Kayla and began stroking again with enough force to almost catch up.

"Perfect backstroke flip turn," Darcy murmured.

Alyssa and Darcy took their places as Kayla and Julie finished their second laps. Kayla finished a split second before Julie. Alyssa and Darcy dove in at almost the same moment.

"Go, Darcy!" Stephanie yelled.

Darcy stroked powerfully through the water. She managed to gain half a pool length on Alyssa. Then Alyssa slowed down in her second lap. Stephanie and Mary got into position to dive in.

Darcy stroked down the pool, coming home. She hit the wall, and Stephanie dove. She rose to the surface of the water and swam the breaststroke as fast as she could. She sensed Mary diving in moments later.

Stephanie tried her hardest to keep ahead of Mary. By her return lap, she was feeling tired. Still, she finished a few strokes before Mary. Allie dove into her lane.

"Way to go, Steph!" Darcy yelled as Stephanie

hoisted herself out of the water. "You put us in the lead!"

Rene was getting ready to swim her final lap. Stephanie watched as Mary reached to tag the wall. Rene dove—a split second before Mary's fingers touched the tiles.

"Hey! Rene jumped her start!" Stephanie called to Baxter. "No fair!"

Baxter shook his head. "You're wrong," he said. "That was a clean start."

Stephanie turned to Darcy. "Am I crazy? Or did Rene cheat?"

"It was so close, it's hard to tell," Darcy admitted.

"Well, can we still beat them?" Stephanie asked.

"I don't know," Darcy replied. "You started way too late, Steph. You should have hit the water the same instant I touched the wall."

"Well, why didn't you tell me that before?" Stephanie asked.

"I thought you already knew that," Darcy replied.

"I didn't!" Stephanie shook her head. "You know I'm only a beginner, Darcy. You make it sound like it's all my fault."

"It's nobody's fault, okay? Next time, I'll tell you everything you should do."

"Great," Stephanie muttered. "Rene cheated and

gets away with it, and I get blamed for doing the wrong thing!"

"Let's forget it, Steph." Darcy turned her attention back to the pool.

Stephanie turned too. "Come on, Allie. Give it everything you've got," she called. "It's up to you now!"

Allie pulled herself down the lane. Rene was a lap ahead, swimming with fantastic speed.

Stephanie looked closer. "I don't believe it!" She groaned. "Allie's breathing every other stroke! Now we'll lose for sure!"

"She's a beginner, too," Darcy pointed out. "She'll get better."

"Yeah, but when?" Stephanie asked.

Rene finished three body lengths ahead of Allie. The race was over—and the Flamingoes had won.

"Yes!" Rene screeched. The other Flamingoes jumped up and down, hugging and squealing. Baxter grinned. "Great job, guys," he told them all.

"Remember—this was only a practice race," Darcy called.

"We know!" Rene gloated. "I can't wait till we beat you for real—in front of everyone we know!"

CHAPTER
7

◆ ◂ ◆ ◆

"No way I'm wearing a shower cap to the pool for a whole day," Stephanie declared.

"Me either," Kayla agreed. "We have to beat those Flamingoes!"

Allie spread a thick coat of cream cheese icing on the carrot cake she had made and lifted the cake onto a glass cake dish.

It was Saturday evening. Stephanie, Allie, and Kayla were gathered in Allie's kitchen, getting ready for Anna's birthday party.

"Baxter is amazing. Since he came along, the Flamingoes are getting better every day," Kayla said. "If this keeps up, we won't have any chance of winning."

"That's no way to talk!" Stephanie replied. "We'll just have to work harder. We have six days left. We'll practice every single day, twice a day, until the race."

"*Twice* a day?" Allie asked. "That sounds like an awful lot."

"Not really," Kayla told her. "We'd have to practice that much for any real swim team."

"Yeah. Twice might not even be enough," Stephanie said. "We might need an evening session, too."

"Let's keep to one session a day, and see what happens," Kayla suggested.

"I'm for that," Allie agreed.

"Okay, okay, calm down," Stephanie said. "We'll try one long practice a day, after camp—for now. We'll be stronger next week, and *then* we can add extra sessions."

Kayla glanced at her watch. "Wow. It's almost eight o'clock," she said. "Shouldn't Anna be here by now?"

"Soon," Allie said.

Stephanie looked at her watch, too. Eight o'clock on Saturday night. Date night. She couldn't help wondering if Rick was out on a date—with Rene.

No, she told herself. *I refuse to worry about Rick all night!*

"Listen, guys," Kayla said. "I've been dying to

talk to you about Anna. I still can't believe she lives in a really rundown house."

"I know," Allie said. "I just can't believe she let us think she lives in a mansion."

Kayla nodded. "I thought she was so rich. But I guess she must be kind of poor."

"When you think about it, she hardly ever wears any new clothes," Allie said.

"I thought it was just her style," Stephanie added. "I thought she liked dressing the way she does."

"She might," Allie said.

"Or she might wear those old clothes because she can't afford better ones," Kayla replied.

Allie gasped. "You guys—remember that day when we went for ice cream sundaes, and Anna only had water?"

"Yeah. She said she was cutting down on sweets," Stephanie said.

"But what if that was just an excuse?" Allie looked worried. "What if she couldn't afford to buy a sundae?"

"Poor Anna," Kayla added. "I feel so bad for her. She must be poor. Otherwise, why did she lie to us about her house and all?"

"I wish there was some way we could help her," Stephanie said. "But at least we're giving her a birthday present."

"Yeah, I'm glad we're chipping in to buy her something," Allie said. "Darcy should be at the mall now, looking for a present. I just hope Darcy gets here before Anna does." Allie went to the refrigerator and lifted out a huge bowl of taco sauce. "Let's set out the food before they both get here."

"I'll help." Kayla pulled out tortilla chips, popcorn, and the other snacks they'd all brought. Stephanie helped arrange them on platters.

There was a knock at the back door, and Anna stepped inside. "Hi, guys!" she called.

"Happy birthday!" Allie, Stephanie, and Kayla cheered.

"Thanks!" Anna glanced around the huge kitchen in amazement. "Wow. This is an incredible kitchen."

"Oh, it's not so much," Allie said quickly. "It just has the usual stuff. Cabinets, sink, stove . . ."

"Yeah, but everything looks so new. It's all so white and shiny!" Anna gaped. "I can't believe that only three people live here. This kitchen is *huge*. In fact, your whole house is huge. Even bigger than Kayla's!"

Kayla lived in a lovely old Victorian house that was painted pale, pretty colors. She and her sister each had their own rooms—big, comfortable rooms.

"Well, I'm sure your house is nice and cozy."

Allie flushed. "I mean, I, uh—" She stopped awkwardly.

"Oh, well, sure it is," Anna said. "Real nice."

"Or it will be, when you're done fixing it up, right?" Kayla added.

"Not that it needs fixing," Stephanie quickly added. "I mean, of course, we've never even seen your house. We—"

The kitchen door flew open and Darcy burst into the room. Her smile spread from ear to ear.

"You guys!" she yelled. "Sorry I'm late! But you'll never believe what I just heard!" She turned to Stephanie. "Steph, you are positively going to love this!"

"Love what?" Stephanie asked. "What did you hear?"

"Okay," Darcy said, catching her breath and flopping into a chair. "Get this. I was in the mall, when who should I see but Alyssa and Mary. They were walking right in front of me—and talking about Rick and Rene!"

Stephanie paled. "I'm not sure I do want to hear this."

"Trust me—you do," Darcy told her. She leaned forward in her chair. "They were talking about the lifeguards' cookout. And I found out"—Darcy paused for effect—"that Rick didn't really kiss Rene!"

Stephanie stared at Darcy. "What do you mean? I *saw* them kiss!"

"Yes! But you didn't know why! It was a dare!" Darcy exclaimed. "They were playing a game of truth or dare. Rick took a dare and lost. He *had* to kiss Rene!" Darcy collapsed back in her chair. She beamed at Stephanie.

"Wow! Steph, that is so cool!" Anna exclaimed. "He didn't want to kiss Rene. He *had* to!"

"He liked you all along!" Kayla cried. "This is great!"

"Darcy, it is so lucky you found out," Allie added. "It changes everything!"

"Does it?" Stephanie asked.

Allie and Darcy exchanged puzzled looks. "Well, of course," Darcy said. "It means Rick never liked Rene."

"But it's too late," Stephanie told them. "Don't you see? I blew it! I got all jealous and wouldn't take his calls, and then we had that fight, and Rick got mad that I spied on him. It doesn't matter about Rene now."

"Hold on," Allie told her. "This *does* matter. You can fix things between you. All you have to do is tell Rick you're sorry about spying on him and that you really like him."

"That's crazy!" Kayla shook her head at Stephanie. "You can't just *tell* a boy that you like him."

"Who says?" Darcy demanded.

"My mom. And I've read it in magazines, too," Kayla replied. "The girl has to play hard to get."

Allie popped a taco into her mouth. "That is so lame," she said with her mouth full. "Guys don't care about dumb stuff like that. Especially not a guy like Rick. And especially not if he still likes Stephanie as much as she likes him."

"Well, *I* think it's a big mistake," Kayla said.

"It's Stephanie's decision," Allie told her.

Everyone turned to look at Stephanie. She made herself a taco, stalling for time. "I'm not sure what to do," she finally admitted.

"You don't have to decide right this minute," Darcy pointed out. "You have all night to think about it."

"But you should decide soon," Kayla said. "You should fix things with Rick now—before Rene really gets her claws into him."

"Well, that *is* true," Stephanie agreed.

Now how do I decide what to do? she wondered. "I'll figure something out," she said. "Later. Right now, let's start the party." She grabbed a platter of food. "Let's take this stuff downstairs."

Everyone grabbed something, and they hurried down the stairs to the family room. It was big and bright and comfortable. Kayla, Anna, and Allie shared the overstuffed green couch. Stephanie pulled up a big wicker armchair. Darcy threw her-self onto a green leather recliner.

They finished eating, and then Allie lit the can-dles on the birthday cake. They all sang "Happy Birthday," and Anna opened her present—a do-it-yourself tie-dye kit and a pretty pair of bead ear-rings to go with it.

"I love this! Thanks, you guys," Anna said.

"I wish it was more," Allie told her. She ex-changed a look of concern with Stephanie.

"These gifts are plenty," Anna replied. "I love them!"

"You know, I saw a bright purple sweatshirt at the mall the other day. It would be perfect with your black hair," Stephanie told her. "I'll buy it for you tomorrow."

"What? Don't, Stephanie." Anna shook her head. "I don't need any more presents."

"It wasn't expensive. Let me get it for you," Stephanie begged.

"Yeah, I'll chip in, too," Darcy offered. Kayla and Allie nodded.

"Cut it out, you guys," Anna said. "You're em-barrassing me. I don't need anything else. I wouldn't even take it."

"Really?" Stephanie asked.

"Absolutely. No more gifts." Anna was firm.

"Well. If you're sure," Stephanie said.

"I'm sure. You gave me plenty." Anna paused. "But I do want more cake. Okay?"

"Of course! Take thirds!" Allie cried.

Anna laughed and helped herself to more cake. Soon everyone was laughing and talking about other things.

Stephanie glanced at the clock. Nine-fifteen. *What is Rick doing now?* she wondered.

She just couldn't stop thinking about him. Should she tell him how much she liked him? But how?

She imagined a thousand different ways to tell him how she felt. The only thing she *couldn't* imagine was what he might say to her.

Could he still like me? she wondered. *Or is he too mad about me spying on him?*

Or worse, had he actually started to like Rene for real?

There's only one way to find out, Stephanie thought. *I have to do what Allie said. I have to tell him how I feel.*

Stephanie stared at the phone in the family room. She could call Rick now—but the thought made her too nervous. How could she possibly say the right things? No, calling was too risky. She had to come up with a better idea.

Late that night, when everyone else was sleeping, Stephanie wiggled out of her sleeping bag. She tiptoed across the darkened family room, careful not to awaken her friends.

She crept up the stairs and went into Allie's room. She turned on the desk lamp and sat down. She pulled a piece of light purple stationery and Allie's favorite purple pen out of her desk.

Stephanie sat staring at the paper for a long time. She finally started to write. About two seconds later she crumpled up the paper. She started again and again.

Maybe I'm making this harder than it has to be, she thought. After all, she was usually a pretty good writer. She tried to remember all the writing tips she had ever learned, like, "Write about what you know," and "Keep it simple."

She took a deep breath and tried again:

Dear Rick,

I realize now that spying on you at the cookout was a mistake. A big mistake.

I am really, really sorry.

You may not believe this, but I only did it because I like you more than I ever liked any boy before.

If you like me, even a little, couldn't we start over again? What do you say?

Stephanie put down her pen and read over what she'd written. It seemed like the best letter yet. It said exactly how she felt.

But how should she sign it? She bit her lip. Could she possibly write, "Love, Stephanie"?

"Yours truly" was too polite. "Sincerely" sounded too stuffy and formal. She could sign it, "Waiting to hear from you soon." But what if Rick thought she was demanding that he write her back? And what if he hated to write letters?

Stephanie stared at the note in agony. Finally she took a deep breath and signed:

Love, Stephanie

Before she could change her mind, she folded the paper and stuffed it into a matching purple envelope. She licked the sticky, sweet glue and sealed it tight.

Tomorrow she would deliver the letter to Rick. He would know she was sorry about the way she acted in the food court. He would know exactly how she felt about him.

And then all she could do was wait to see how *he* felt about *her*.

CHAPTER
8

◆ ◀ ▪ ◆

Early the next morning, the girls finished an enormous pancake breakfast.

Anna peeked at her watch. "Wow, I need to head home right now. I promised I'd help my mom around the house today."

"My mom can drop you when she takes us to the pool," Allie offered. "We're going in a few minutes."

"Oh, no! I can't. I mean, um, I'd rather take the bus," Anna replied. "I'll be late if I don't go right this minute, and the bus is really fast." Anna grabbed her backpack.

"Well, okay, if you'd rather not," Allie said, exchanging a knowing look with Stephanie. "Do you have all your stuff?"

"I think so." Anna checked inside her backpack. "Here's my presents and . . . oh, no."

"What's wrong?" Stephanie asked.

"I forgot my wallet." Anna shook her head. "I was so rushed when I left my house last night. . . ."

"No problem!" Allie ran to grab her own wallet. "I can lend you money. How much do you need?" She pulled out a few crumpled dollar bills.

"I have money, too," Stephanie said. She dug through her backpack—and saw the purple envelope inside.

Rick's letter! I can't wait to give it to him today, she thought. *I wonder what he'll say when he reads it?*

"Well, I feel dumb, but okay." Anna accepted Allie's money. "I'll pay you back next time I see you."

"Don't bother," Allie replied.

Anna gave her a curious look. "Of course I'll pay you back."

"It's only bus fare," Allie protested. "I mean, uh, it's your birthday today, isn't it? So I should treat."

"Allie, I can pay you back," Anna insisted.

"Whatever," Allie said.

Anna checked her watch again and lifted her backpack. "I think I'd better *run.* Thanks, Allie. See you guys later!"

Allie and the others waited until Anna had

rushed out the door. Then they all began talking at once.

"Do you think she suspected anything?" Stephanie asked.

"She acted sort of suspicious when you offered her bus fare," Allie said. "I think she knows that we know she doesn't have a lot of money."

"How would she know that?" Darcy responded.

"She would if she saw you spying on her house," Kayla pointed out.

"I'm sure she didn't see us," Allie said. "This is awful. I feel like a sneak again, and I don't know what to do about it."

"We'll figure something out," Kayla said. She sighed.

"Anyway, we should get an early start, too," Darcy told them.

"Right," Kayla agreed. "It's great that we don't have camp today. We can get in hours of practice."

"We're not going to swim all day, are we?" Allie asked. "I'd like to actually do something fun this afternoon."

"No problem," Darcy assured her. "Right, Steph? Steph?" she repeated.

"Huh?" Stephanie was staring at Rick's letter. She glanced up. "Oh, uh, sure. Let's go."

As soon as they reached the community center,

Darcy, Kayla, and Allie headed toward the locker room.

"I'll be right there," Stephanie told them. "I need to do something first." She nearly raced over to the pool. She still wasn't sure how she would get her letter to Rick. She wanted to make sure he received it, but she didn't want to be there when he read it. To her relief, Mike was alone in the lifeguard chair.

"Hey—is Rick around now?" she asked.

"He's here somewhere," Mike told her. "I just saw him."

Stephanie spotted Rick's backpack sitting on the pavement near the chair. It was red, with Rick's initials in black: R.S. She slipped the purple envelope out of her backpack and tucked it into the front pocket of Rick's backpack.

There! Rick will read my letter, and then everything will be all right between us! she thought. *I hope!*

"Listen, Mike—when Rick comes back, would you tell him I left a note for him in his backpack?" Stephanie asked.

"Sure thing," Mike answered.

Stephanie hurried to the locker room and changed into her suit in record time. She felt happier than she had in days! She raced to join the others.

The pool was crowded for early Sunday morning. But at least the lap lanes were free. And they could use both lanes—until the Flamingoes arrived.

Stephanie sneaked a glance at the lifeguard chair. Still no Rick. She almost giggled. Rick was about to read her letter! He would know how she felt about him! The thought was exciting—and a little terrifying, too.

"Okay, you guys!" Darcy called. "Let's each work on our relay strokes for a while. Then we'll practice our starting dives."

Everyone dove into the water. Stephanie tried hard to keep her mind on practice, but she kept checking for Rick after each stroke. They finished four practice laps. Stephanie glanced toward the lifeguard chair for about the fiftieth time.

Why hadn't Rick come back yet? she wondered.

They moved on to diving practice, then swam six practice relays. Then they climbed out of the pool to practice diving again. The whole time, Stephanie watched for Rick. She was having a hard time keeping her mind on swimming.

The Flamingoes arrived with Baxter. Stephanie and her friends climbed out of the water for a rest. The Flamingoes dove into the pool, and Baxter soon had them racing against his stopwatch. He called out their times, and they were faster than ever. For the first time that day, Stephanie forgot about Rick. She stared at the Flamingoes as they cut through the water at top speed.

"Looking great!" Baxter exclaimed.

"Great? They're unreal!" Allie gaped at them in disbelief. "They're even faster than before."

"I know," Stephanie replied. "We're not going to beat them at this rate."

"Hey, let's try a few practice relays and time our laps, too," Darcy suggested. "Maybe we're better than we think."

"Trust me, we're not," Stephanie told her. "It's too bad we don't have a coach like Baxter."

"Excuse me? I thought *I* was a pretty good coach," Darcy said.

"You are," Stephanie said. "But let's face it, Darce—you're no Baxter. Look at the way he has them running practice dives, one after the other. We've never even tried that."

"Well, we can't try it now. I need a break," Allie complained. "I'm worn out from diving."

"Me too," Kayla said. "Let's get some lunch."

"Sounds good. You coming, Stephanie?" Darcy asked.

"In a minute," Stephanie replied. She glanced at the lifeguard chair again. Rick wasn't back, and now Mike was gone, too. Alyssa sat on the chair, fixing her lip gloss. Stephanie checked for Rick's backpack. It wasn't there!

Oh, no! Rick took his backpack and left, and I missed him! She could have kicked herself.

"You guys go ahead," Stephanie told Darcy. "I'll meet you at the snack shack in a minute." She waited until they were far away. Then she hurried over to the lifeguard's chair.

"Hey, Alyssa! Did you see Rick?" Stephanie demanded.

"Not that it's any of your business, but Rick went home sick," Alyssa said. "Sandy asked me to fill in for him for the rest of the day."

Stephanie got a sinking feeling. "You mean, he won't be back at *all?*"

"I guess." Alyssa shrugged. "How should I know?"

"Thanks a lot," Stephanie muttered.

Now how will I know if he read my letter? she wondered.

Stephanie sighed and headed toward the snack shack. On the way, she passed a garbage can—and stopped short. A purple envelope was lying on top of the trash!

She quickly pulled it out. It was the envelope that had held her letter! And it was torn open.

Rick must have read my letter before he left, she thought. *He knows I'm sorry about the cookout and about our fight in the food court. And he knows how I feel about him. Then why didn't he at least come over to say good-bye?*

But Rick was sick, she reminded herself.

Sure, that's it, she thought. *He didn't feel well. That's why he didn't stop to talk to me. But I bet he'll call me tonight. And I can't wait to talk to him!*

CHAPTER
9

◆ ◀ ◆ ◆

Stephanie headed home. The instant she got inside, she checked the phone machine. But Rick hadn't called. She stared at the phone. "Ring!" she ordered. Nothing happened. Her heart sank.

He didn't call before dinner, during dinner, or after dinner. By nine o'clock, she was losing hope. She dragged herself upstairs to get ready for bed.

Riiiing!

"Stephanie, phone!" D.J. called up the stairs.

Please let it be Rick, she thought.

"I'll take it up here!" Stephanie raced down the hall to her father's upstairs office. She pounced on the phone. "Hello?"

"Hi, Steph," Darcy said. "It's me."

"And me," Allie added. Allie had three-way calling on her phone.

"Oh." Stephanie slumped in disappointment.

"Gee, don't sound so excited," Darcy teased.

"Sorry, guys. It's just that I was hoping Rick would call me."

"No offense, but why would he call you?" Darcy asked.

Stephanie hesitated. "I wrote him a letter to apologize," she admitted. "And to tell him how much I like him."

"You didn't!" Darcy sounded shocked. "And he hasn't called yet?"

"No. Do you think it was a mistake?" Stephanie asked.

"Well, if he read it and didn't call . . ." Darcy's voice trailed off.

Stephanie thought of her letter and cringed. *Why did I ever sign it with "love"?*

"What should I do, you guys?" Stephanie asked.

"Maybe you need to find an excuse to talk to him about something else," Allie told her. "Then you can straighten everything out."

"Great. So give me an excuse to call him," Stephanie said.

"Well, you could ask him to watch our next swim practice," Allie suggested.

Stephanie gasped. "Allie—that gives me a great

idea! I'll ask him to be our official Club Stephanie personal trainer!''

"Uh, why would you do that?" Darcy asked. "I'm our coach!"

"I know, but think about it, Darce," Stephanie said. "Rick is a terrific swimmer. And he knows a lot about coaching. And you're trying to do two things—coach us and practice yourself. It might be better for the team if Rick takes over.''

"I guess that might be true," Darcy admitted.

"Yeah. Rick can be our coach, and Stephanie can find out how he feels about her," Allie added.

"Right," Stephanie replied.

"Do you have the nerve to call him tonight?" Allie asked.

"I don't know, but I'll find out," Stephanie answered. "I better hang up now—it's getting late. See you in the morning, guys." Allie and Darcy said good-bye. Stephanie hung up the phone. She stared at it for a moment.

She took a deep breath and picked up the receiver again. "Hi, Rick," she mumbled, practicing her phone call. "It's Stephanie. Listen, I had a great idea! You should coach the Club Stephanie swim team!"

It sounded totally lame. She slammed down the phone.

It's getting way too late to call, anyway, she told

herself. *And Rick did go home sick today. He might already be asleep, and I don't want to wake him.*

It would definitely be best to wait until morning.

Sun glinted off the pool. Stephanie stopped in her tracks. Rick was sitting in the lifeguard chair!

Stephanie checked her watch. She had only five minutes before camp began. But that was time enough to ask Rick to be their coach. And from the way he answered, Stephanie would know if they were friends again—or not.

She took a deep breath for courage, then approached the chair. "Um, hi, Rick," she said.

"Hi." Rick looked grumpy. But maybe he was still feeling sick.

"How are you feeling today?" Stephanie asked.

Rick barely looked at her. "Okay, I guess. I mean, I came to work, didn't I?"

Stephanie cringed.

Oh, no! He sounds really mad at me. He hated my letter. I did come on too strong! Kayla was right, Stephanie thought.

"Well, listen—I need to ask you a really big favor." Stephanie gulped. "Would you coach Club Stephanie for our relay race? We really need help, especially now that Baxter's helping the Flamingoes."

Rick didn't answer right away. "Why would you want *me* to coach you?" he finally asked.

"Well, um, because you're a great swimmer," Stephanie stammered.

Rick kept his eyes on the pool. "Don't you think that would be a little"—he paused and cleared his throat—"uncomfortable?"

Not more uncomfortable than I feel right now! Stephanie thought. "No, it wouldn't be uncomfortable for me," she replied.

"Well, it would be uncomfortable for *me*," Rick said. He flushed a dark red and then looked away.

"Oh." Stephanie stood there, not knowing what to do next. Rick wouldn't look at her. And he obviously didn't want to talk to her—at all.

"Well, I guess that's that," Stephanie finally said.

"Guess so," Rick answered.

Stephanie headed for the picnic area. *Talk about bad ideas!* she thought. *What a total disaster!*

The Club Stephanie campers were already hard at work on their flag projects. Allie, Kayla, and Darcy rushed over to Stephanie.

"Well, how did it go?" Allie demanded. "What did Rick say?"

"Will he coach us?" Darcy asked.

Stephanie shook her head. She felt close to tears. "No. He won't."

"Why?" Anna asked. "What did he say about your letter?"

"He didn't say anything about it." Stephanie ran her hand through her hair. "He just seemed kind of angry."

"That doesn't make sense," Kayla said. "I mean, how could a love letter make you angry? He should be flattered you like him so much!"

"That's what I thought." Stephanie bit her lip.

"Of course, it would make him uncomfortable if he didn't love you back," Anna blurted.

"Anna!" Kayla's eyes opened in shock. "Don't say that!"

"She might as well say it," Stephanie told her. "It's what I'm thinking. It's probably what you're all thinking."

Kayla stared down at the ground. Darcy and Allie shifted their weight from one foot to the other.

"Don't worry, you guys," Stephanie told them. "I couldn't feel worse than I already do."

Camp went all right. But Stephanie felt a little weird when it was time to head to the pool for the kids' swimming session. How could she face Rick? But Rick wasn't there when she arrived.

Safe—for now, Stephanie thought.

The kids had a great time playing a game of ring toss and water tag. Then it was time for snacks and arts and crafts. Stephanie had to work hard to keep her mind on the activities. All she could think about was Rick and her letter.

I wish I never wrote that stupid letter, she thought. *I should have listened to Kayla!*

Finally camp was over for the day. Stephanie breathed a sigh of relief as they waved good-bye to the last camper. "Let's grab a snack," she suggested.

"Sounds good." Anna stretched. "How about pizza?"

Stephanie and Allie exchanged looks of concern. "Well, um, were you planning on buying a snack today?" Stephanie asked.

"Huh?" Anna looked surprised.

"Well, I mean, maybe the rest of us should get right to practice," Stephanie said.

"But you were the one who suggested a snack," Anna pointed out.

"Oh, I know, but, um—" Stephanie stopped.

"You are acting so weird." Anna shook her head. "We all want pizza, so let's go." She led the way to the snack shack, and they lined up at the counter. "Slices all around?" she asked. "Though I could eat an *entire* pizza. I'm starving!"

"We could order extra slices for you," Kayla offered.

"I was kidding," Anna said. "But let's order a

whole pie instead of slices. You get more for your money that way—three more slices for only twenty cents extra."

"That sounds smart," Stephanie said, giving the others a meaningful look.

"Right! And you can take any leftover slices home," Kayla told Anna.

"Why would I want to do that?" Anna gave them a strange look. "You guys are the ones training hard. You're the ones who need to stoke up on heavy carbs."

"I guess," Kayla muttered.

Anna shrugged. She placed the order, and they waited.

"Anna is right, actually," Darcy began. "We should be eating like athletes in training."

"It wouldn't hurt," Stephanie agreed. "We should eat extra carbs, and get extra rest. In fact, we should probably get to bed early tonight. Then we can add in an extra practice in the morning tomorrow, before camp."

Allie groaned. "Do we have to?"

The pizza was ready. "We owe two dollars each," Anna said.

Stephanie pulled two dollars and fifty cents from her wallet. "Here—let me pay a little extra."

Allie glanced at Stephanie. "Here's the same from me."

"Me too," Darcy said. She and Kayla also paid two dollars and fifty cents.

"All paid," Stephanie said. She slid the money toward the cashier.

"Wait, you guys," Anna said. "I haven't chipped in yet!"

"Don't worry about it. It's on us," Stephanie offered.

"You guys don't have to pay for me," Anna argued. "I have money."

"Yeah, but, uh, we're in training, not you," Stephanie said. "So we should pay."

"And it was just your birthday," Allie added.

Anna looked at the others as if they were crazy. "Okay. But I'll treat next time."

They found an empty table and divided up the pizza. Stephanie slipped on a new turquoise headband to keep her hair out of the way before taking her first bite.

"Great color headband!" Anna bit into her pizza. "Is it new?"

"Yeah," Stephanie said.

"I could use some new headbands myself," Anna commented.

"Really?" Stephanie sat up straighter. "Why don't you take this one? Actually, I think it's a better color for you." Stephanie pulled the headband off and held it out to Anna.

Anna laughed. "I don't want your new headband! I just think it's pretty."

"Then you should borrow it," Stephanie insisted.
"That's what we always do. Right, Allie?"

"Uh, right," Allie said. "We swap clothes and
stuff all the time. Take it, Anna."

"No! Would you stop trying to give me things?"
What's wrong with you guys, anyway?" She stood,
carrying her slice of pizza. "I've got to run. Have
fun at practice. See you all tomorrow." She hurried away.

Stephanie waited a few seconds, then motioned
for everyone to lean closer. "I just got the best
idea!" she exclaimed. "I know exactly what we
should do to help Anna!"

CHAPTER
10

◆ ◀ ◆ ◆

"Hi, everybody," Anna called early the next morning. "Did you guys get here early for another swim practice?" She slid onto a bench at the picnic table where the other girls were sitting.

"Yeah, we've been here for hours," Stephanie replied. She glanced at Anna's outfit: ragged cut-offs and a black polo shirt.

"Are you guys getting any better in the relay or . . ." Anna's voice trailed off. She stared at an enormous stack of clothes piled on the center of the table. "What is all this stuff?" she asked.

"Clothes!" Kayla announced

"For you," Darcy added.

Anna reached into the pile and lifted up a yellow

linen sundress. There was a funny look on her face. "Where did these clothes come from?" she asked.

"Oh, that dress used to be Darcy's," Stephanie said.

"But I only wore it a few times," Darcy quickly added. "In fact, I only got it a few months ago."

"Then why are you giving it to me?" Anna asked.

"Well, you know," Stephanie began. "It's like we said yesterday. We always swap clothes."

"Right," Darcy agreed. "And we decided you should go first today."

Anna put the sundress down on the table. She crossed her arms over her chest. "If we're *all* swapping today, why didn't you guys talk to me about this? I would have brought some clothes, too."

"Because—we wanted it to be a surprise," Stephanie said.

Anna pressed her lips together. "Tell me the truth," she said. "You don't like the way I dress— do you?"

"I love the way you dress!" Stephanie exclaimed.

"Me too!" Kayla added. Allie and Darcy nodded.

Anna shook her head. "I think I embarrass you. You want me to change the way I look. Why else would you try to give me stuff that doesn't look one bit like the clothes I wear?"

"Uh . . . because, um," Stephanie began. She threw Allie a helpless look.

"We just think swapping is fun," Allie said. "And we love the way you dress, Anna. I wish I could dress half as cool as you do."

Anna sat down and took a shaky breath. "If you guys are really my friends, you'll tell me the truth. Do you hate my clothes?"

"No," Stephanie insisted. She put a hand on Anna's shoulder. "We were just trying to help."

"Help?" Anna asked. "Why would I need help?"

"Uh . . ." Stephanie couldn't think of what to say. Allie and Darcy dropped their eyes. For a long moment, nobody spoke.

Finally Allie cleared her throat. "Well, why else would you lie?" she asked.

"I don't lie!" Anna said, looking startled.

Allie and Stephanie exchanged a knowing look. "We saw your house," Stephanie said.

"You what?" Anna stared at her in shock.

"We didn't mean to, but we did, and, uh . . ." Stephanie glanced at Allie for help.

"Well, it isn't exactly how you described it, and so we thought, maybe . . ." Allie stopped too.

"And so you thought that I needed your hand-me-downs!" Anna burst out angrily.

"Don't blame us," Stephanie said. "We didn't mean to insult you or anything."

"No, but you've just been talking about me be-hind my back! You've been saying, poor Anna. What can we do to help her?" Anna's tone made it clear how much she hated that idea.

"It wasn't like that at all," Stephanie began. "We just thought—"

"I know exactly what you thought!" Anna looked embarrassed and angry at the same time.

"It's all right," Darcy told her. "We don't care where you live, or if you're rich or poor—"

"Or how you dress," Allie finished for her. "We just wanted to help you out, and—"

"I don't need your help!" Anna cried. "I—I don't need any of you. Ever again!" She turned and ran.

"Anna!" Stephanie yelled.

"Anna, wait! Come back!" The others shouted, too, but Anna kept going.

Stephanie stared at her friends in dismay. "This time, I think we really, really blew it!"

Camp dragged by that morning. Stephanie felt sick to her stomach the whole time. She could barely stand to see Rick at the pool. It hurt to think about how badly she'd messed up—with Rick *and* Anna.

Finally camp was over for the day. "Let's call Anna," Stephanie suggested after lunch at the snack shack. "Maybe we can convince her to for-give us and come back tomorrow."

"I'm for that," Kayla said. Allie and Darcy agreed. They all hurried over to the pay phone in the clubhouse.

Stephanie dialed. "I got her answering ma-chine," she announced.

"Let's leave our message, anyway," Allie said.

"Okay." Stephanie held the receiver at arm's length. Darcy, Allie, and Kayla crowded close to the pay telephone in the clubhouse.

"We miss you, Anna. Please come back!" they all yelled.

Stephanie pulled back the phone. "Hi, Anna," she said. "It's true. We all really miss you. And we're really, really sorry that we—we did what we did. The kids totally miss you at camp. They're so disappointed that you aren't here to work on their flags for the parade. If you get this message, well, come back. And please forgive us."

Stephanie waited a moment, then hung up.

"We'll try her again later," Kayla said. "Maybe she'll be home, and she'll talk to us then."

"I hope so," Stephanie said. "I really hope so."

Darcy clicked off the stopwatch. "Six minutes, twenty-six seconds," she announced.

"That's great!" Stephanie pulled herself out of

the water. "We knocked thirty seconds off our last time!"

Practice was finally going well that afternoon. "Maybe we *can* beat the Flamingoes!" Stephanie felt a burst of hope.

"Sure we can," Darcy said. "I told you we'd get better."

"Let's take a short break," Kayla suggested. "The Flamingoes have signed up for their practice soon, anyway. Let's come back for more practice when they're done."

"We can't rest now," Stephanie argued. "Our time is finally better. We have to keep it up. Don't forget, the Flamingoes are still faster." She shook her head in frustration. "I just wish I knew what we were doing wrong!"

"We're not doing *anything* wrong," Darcy said. "What's the matter with you, Steph? Our time has improved tons."

"But not enough to *win*," Stephanie argued. "We have got to add more practices."

Darcy rolled her eyes. Kayla groaned.

"Come on, Steph," Allie grumbled. "My mom is starting to complain that she never sees me anymore. I haven't been home for dinner in a week."

"Which is more important? Dinner or beating the Flamingoes?" Stephanie asked.

"Quiet, you guys. Here they come." Kayla nodded toward the other side of the pool. Mary, Alyssa, and Julie dumped their stuff on a chair and pulled on their swim goggles.

"Where's Rene?" Allie wondered.

"She's right behind the others. And she's with Rick," Kayla added.

Stephanie felt her stomach lurch. She and Allie and Darcy all turned to look. Rene handed Rick a stopwatch. Julie handed him a clipboard.

"What is he doing?" Darcy asked. "Where's Baxter?"

"I don't know," Stephanie murmured. "But I have a funny feeling. . . ."

"I've got to find out what's happening." Darcy hurried over to Rick. Stephanie saw them exchange a few words. Darcy raced back.

"You're not going to like this," Darcy began. "Baxter had to leave town to visit a sick relative. And—" She hesitated.

"And what?" Stephanie prompted.

Darcy took a deep breath. "And Rick is the Flamingoes' new swim coach!"

Stephanie stared at Darcy in disbelief. "You mean, he chose the Flamingoes over us?"

"I guess so. Sorry, Steph." Darcy squeezed Stephanie's arm in sympathy.

Stephanie stared blindly at the Flamingoes. Rick nodded at them. "Okay," he said. "Swim a couple of practice laps, any style you choose. Julie, you go first."

Julie dove into the water and sped down the lane. "Great form!" Rick cried. "Keep it up!"

The other Flamingoes were laughing and chatting as they watched Julie swim.

This is it, Stephanie thought. *There's no hope for me now. It's totally over between us.*

"Darcy, there's only one thing left to do," Stephanie said. "We've got to think of a way to totally humiliate those Flamingoes!"

CHAPTER

11

◆ ◀ ◾ ◆

"Maybe we'd better take that break now," Darcy said. "Come on, Steph." She motioned to Kayla and Allie. "Let's just sit until the Flamingoes' practice is over."

Stephanie followed the others through the crowd. The Flamingoes had saved their usual group of chairs arranged around their pink umbrella.

"I hope there's a few empty chairs for us somewhere," Darcy murmured.

"I don't see any," Stephanie replied.

"Hey—Club Stephanie! Wait! I saved some chairs for you guys." Tiffany motioned for Stephanie to stop. Stephanie saw that Tiffany stood guarding five pool chairs.

"Why would you save chairs for . . . ?" Stephanie began to ask. Then Tiffany grinned and stepped aside.

A giant green shower cap was taped to the back of one chair. Across the cap the words STE-PHANIE TANNER—LOSER were printed in tall, black letters.

The Flamingoes all burst into laughter. Everyone nearby turned to stare at Stephanie. Stephanie turned her head—and saw Rick watching, too.

"I don't believe this!" Stephanie murmured.

"Forget it, Steph," Allie told her.

"Yeah, ignore them," Kayla added.

I will not let them see me getting upset, Stephanie told herself.

"Forget the break," she snapped at Darcy. "We can't afford to goof off now. Let's get back in the water and show the Flamingoes what we can really do!"

"Uh, maybe now's not the best time for that," Darcy told her.

"Now *is* the time! The picnic is Saturday!" Stephanie exclaimed. "We only have four days left to practice!"

Darcy glanced at Allie and Kayla. She lowered her voice. "Listen, Steph, we know you're upset about Rick and the dumb shower cap and all. But taking it out on us won't help."

"Well, someone had better help," Stephanie murmured. "Because you can't."

"I heard that! What do you mean?" Darcy scowled.

"It means that we're running out of time. And I don't think we can count on you to help enough." Stephanie felt her voice rising in panic, but she couldn't seem to stop it. "I'm having trouble swimming a straight line. Allie will never be a strong swimmer. You and Kayla are the best swimmers we've got, but you both seem to be stuck in slow motion or something. In other words, Darcy, our team is *pathetic!*"

"You better calm down," Darcy warned.

"Yeah, Steph, give us a break," Allie added.

"I'll calm down when we get the help we need," Stephanie shot back.

Darcy put her hands on her hips. "Since you know *exactly* what we're doing wrong, why don't you tell us what we can do to change things?"

"Fine, I will," Stephanie said. "First of all, it would help if *you* were more strict, Darcy."

"This is only a race against the Flamingoes," Darcy pointed out. "It's *not* the Olympics. And it's not life or death. We can take a break to relax sometimes."

"We can relax *after* we win," Stephanie told her.

Darcy's eyes narrowed. "You know, I'm doing the best that I can."

"Well, it isn't really good enough, is it?" Stephanie blurted.

"Whoa!" Darcy said. "Is that what you think?"

"I think we don't have much chance of winning on Saturday," Stephanie said. "And we'll never win if we don't get even more serious. Like, adding more practices."

"Now you've really lost it," Darcy told her. "More? How could we practice *more?*"

"We could start a couple of hours earlier for the next three mornings, that's how," Stephanie said. "We could practice three solid hours before Club Stephanie even starts."

Kayla stepped in between Stephanie and Darcy. "Look, Steph, I want to beat the Flamingoes, too," Kayla began. "But I can't swim that much extra. No one can!"

Allie nodded. "Steph, you've got to stop making such a huge deal out of this race. I mean, what does it really prove if the Flamingoes swim faster than we do?"

"It proves everything!" Stephanie said. "It proves that we're as good as Rene. It proves they can't make us look ridiculous in front of the whole pool."

"Steph, wait a minute," Allie tried to say.

"We have to win. We have to!" Stephanie declared.

"You know what?" Darcy asked. "I'm going home. I think we all need a break. I don't even want to *think* about swimming anymore today."

Stephanie folded her arms across her chest. "That is a really bad attitude," she told Darcy. "If we lose on Saturday, it's going to be all your fault."

"That's enough, you guys," Allie said.

"Please don't fight," Kayla added.

Darcy yanked her goggles off her head. "Well, you don't have to worry about my attitude anymore," she snapped. "Because I just decided something. I'm not your coach anymore. In fact, I'm not going to swim in the stupid race!"

"Darce—" Stephanie started.

"Forget it," Darcy yelled. "I've had enough. I quit!" She stormed off, heading to the locker room in the clubhouse.

Allie turned to Stephanie. "Don't you think you went a little overboard?"

"No way!" Stephanie insisted. "Darcy knows I'm right. You'll see—she'll show up at practice early tomorrow. She knows we need the extra time. And she'll be the first to thank me when we win."

90

Allie sighed. "I don't know about that. Remember, Steph, there are more important things than beating the Flamingoes."

"You're wrong," Stephanie told her. "Nothing is more important than beating the Flamingoes. Nothing."

CHAPTER
12

♦ ◂ ▸ ♦

"Is she here yet?" Kayla plopped down on a lounge chair next to Stephanie. She wrapped an enormous blue beach towel around her shoulders. The early morning light was just starting to hit the pool.

Stephanie glanced at the clock on the clubhouse wall. 7:10. She, Allie, and Kayla had already practiced for over an hour. There was no sign of Darcy.

"She'll show," Stephanie said. "I'm sure she's calmed down a lot since yesterday."

"Well, I'm not," Allie said. "Darcy was really mad. And she wasn't wrong, either. You went too far, Steph. You really should call and say you're sorry."

"Allie's right," Kayla agreed. "Darcy did a pretty good job as our coach. You can't blame her for all our problems. Call her, Steph. Please?"

"Okay, okay, I'll call." Stephanie grabbed her wallet and headed toward the clubhouse. She slipped some coins into the pay phone and dialed Darcy's number.

"Hello?" Darcy answered right away.

"Darce? It's me," Stephanie replied. "Listen, I'm sorry for yesterday. I was hoping you'd change your mind and come to early practice this morning."

"*I* was hoping *you* would stop being so bossy!" Darcy replied.

"I'm not being bossy," Stephanie told her. "I'm just trying to make sure that we win."

Darcy snorted. "I've got a news flash for you. You don't win races by running around yelling at people."

"Oh, I'm really glad I apologized," Stephanie said sarcastically.

"Don't worry about it," Darcy snapped. "It wasn't a great apology. And I'm not coming to practice until you chill out. I'm sick of hearing about how we have to beat the Flamingoes."

"I don't believe you. We *have* to beat them!" Stephanie exclaimed. "Do you really want to hang out at the pool in a shower cap?"

"Right now I don't want to hang out at the pool at all," Darcy retorted. "Thanks to you, it's no fun anymore. And neither is camp. So have fun at Club Stephanie today—without me. 'Cause I'm not coming!" She slammed down the phone.

Stephanie stared at the receiver in shock. Then she slowly hung up the phone and headed back to the pool.

"What happened? Is Darcy coming back?" Kayla asked.

Stephanie shook her head. "Nope. Sorry, guys."

Allie sighed. "Well, I guess I'm splitting as soon as camp is over today."

"You're not staying for afternoon practice?" Stephanie asked.

"What's the point?" Allie asked. "The three of us can't swim a four-person relay. Unless Darcy comes back, the race is off."

"But . . ." Stephanie blinked. She stared at Allie and Kayla. "But we can't just quit. We have to do *something*," she protested.

"Like what?" Allie asked. "There's hardly any time until the race."

Kayla shrugged. "Face it, Steph. It's over."

Stephanie pushed a glob of coleslaw around on her plate.

"What's wrong, Steph?" Danny asked her.

Stephanie glanced at her dad, sitting across from her at the dinner table. "I just don't have much of an appetite."

"Worn out from too much swimming?" D.J. asked.

Stephanie slumped in her chair. "We're not practicing anymore," she told her family. "Darcy quit the team yesterday. She won't coach us or swim. So the race is off."

"What?" Joey stared at Stephanie. "Darcy never seemed like a quitter before."

"She isn't a quitter," Stephanie admitted. "It's kind of all my fault."

Danny frowned. "Your fault? What do you mean?"

Stephanie took a deep breath, then told her family everything that happened—at swimming practice. She left out all the stuff about Rick and Anna. That was *too* embarrassing to discuss in front of everyone.

"Wow," Becky said. "It really does sound like you overreacted. I feel bad for Darcy."

"You and Darcy have been friends for a long time," Danny said. "I'm sure you can find some way to make up."

"I hope you're right," Stephanie said.

After dinner, Stephanie loaded the dishwasher.

As she slipped in the last few dishes, the phone rang.

"Steph, listen!" It was Kayla. "I think I know how to get Darcy back on the team. I was thinking, what we really need now is some help with our flip turns. It saves tons of time if you can do a really tight one. What we need is a flip-turn expert."

"Sounds great," Stephanie agreed. "But who could we get?"

"I was thinking of Cody," Kayla explained. "The flip turn is his special talent."

"Yeah, but would he really do it?" Stephanie felt a burst of hope. "Could you call him and ask?"

"I already did," Kayla admitted. "He wants to help. My uncle will drive him over to the pool tomorrow. He'll meet us at the snack shack at two."

"Not until two?" Stephanie asked. "We only have one practice left. We need every minute we can get."

"I know it's a little late. But we can stay late, too," Kayla said. "And one practice with Cody James is worth a week of practice with anyone else."

"Sounds great!" Stephanie said. "This could save us!"

"There's just one problem. . . ." Kayla paused.

"We still need four of us on the team. We have to get Darcy back."

"Oh," Stephanie said. "That *is* a problem."

"Steph, I think you should call her again. We can't win without her," Kayla said.

"I guess," Stephanie replied.

"And you two have got to make up, anyway," Kayla added.

"I know you're right." Stephanie sighed. "I'm just not sure what to say to her."

"You'll think of something," Kayla said. "And speaking of making up—you'll never guess who I saw at the library this afternoon. Anna!"

Stephanie felt a jolt go through her stomach. "Did you talk to her? Did she talk to you?"

"No." Kayla sounded disappointed. "I waved at her, but she didn't wave back. She pretended not to see me. I guess she's still mad at us."

Who isn't? Stephanie thought.

"Yeah. Well, thanks a lot for asking Cody to help," Stephanie told Kayla. "I'll call Darcy right now and tell her about it."

"Good luck," Kayla said.

Stephanie dialed Darcy's number. Her phone rang three times and then the answering machine clicked on.

"Hi, you've reached the Powells' house," Darcy's mother's voice announced. "Leave a message after the beep."

Beep!

"Ah, hi, Darcy . . . it's me. Stephanie," Stephanie began.

"I have some good news for you," she went on. "At least, I think it's good news. Well, here it is— Cody agreed to be our new coach, starting tomorrow. But we really, really need you to come back. And—and we miss you. I miss you! I'm so sorry for everything I said. Let's not fight anymore, please?"

Stephanie hung up. Then she remembered that last time she had spoken to Darcy, she said they'd have early practice in the morning. But Cody wasn't coming until two.

Stephanie sighed and hit the redial button. *Beep!*

"Stephanie again. Cody is coming at two. So don't come before then. That is, *if* you decide to come back. Which I really hope you do." Stephanie hung up.

She had tried. Now it was up to Darcy. All she could do was wait.

CHAPTER
13

♦ ◀ ◗ ♦

"Darcy!" Stephanie leaped up and threw her arms around her best friend. "I am so glad you came back!"

"Hey, everybody," Darcy said. "I came as soon as I finished listening to Stephanie's phone messages!"

"This is so great!" Stephanie exclaimed. "Thanks, Darce. I really, really hate fighting with you. And I'm really, really sorry for the things I said, and—"

"Okay, okay!" Darcy laughed, holding up her hands in front of her face. "I get the picture! It feels great to be back. And I kind of wanted to be here to help the kids finish their flags today."

Allie sighed. "We sure could use Anna's help."

"Well, Stephanie got me to come back," Darcy said. "Maybe she could get Anna back, too."

"How about it, Steph?" Kayla turned to her. "Want to give it another try?"

"Okay," Stephanie told her. She dug into her shorts for a quarter. "I'll call Anna again—but don't hold your breath. I have a feeling it will be just one more phone message that doesn't get answered."

Stephanie hurried to the pay phone in the clubhouse and dialed Anna's number. The machine picked up again. Stephanie sighed.

"Hi, this message is for Anna," she began. "It's Stephanie. Listen, I just want you to know again that everyone is sorry about what happened. Please, don't be mad at us! The important thing is that we all miss you. And the kids *really* miss you. And they need your help! They have to finish their flags, and we're all afraid we'll mess them up! Please, please, come back and save us!"

She paused.

"Well, okay, then." She was about to say good-bye when someone picked up the phone.

"Hello? Stephanie?" Anna said.

"Anna!" Stephanie felt a rush of relief. "You're speaking to me!"

"Well, I heard what you said about the flags,"

Anna began. "And I know how excited the kids are about the parade."

"Yeah," Stephanie agreed. "And since making the flags was your idea, we thought you should help finish them."

"I guess so," Anna said. She was silent for a moment.

"That's not the real reason I called," Stephanie admitted. "Listen, Anna, I'm sorry we tried to give you our clothes and everything. I don't know how to explain what happened," she began. "But—"

"Wait." Anna stopped her. "Let *me* explain."

"You?" Stephanie asked in surprise. "What do you need to explain?"

"Well, the way I acted, running away and all. I was just so embarrassed," Anna said.

"Really? We thought you were mad at *us*, because we spied on you," Stephanie said.

"No." Anna shook her head. "It's just that day at Allie's, I was trying to tell you about my house and all, but you didn't give me a chance. You all kept talking about me having this big, beautiful house, and somehow things got all twisted up. I didn't mean to lie about where I lived."

"I guess we jumped to conclusions, too," Stephanie said. "We thought you didn't have any money, and that's why we kept offering to pay for stuff and give you things."

"Is that why you were all acting so weird?" Anna laughed in relief. "I mean, I'm not rich—but I can usually pay for my own clothes, and snacks, or the bus!"

"Well, we *did* go overboard," Stephanie told her.

"So did I," Anna replied. "Look, I know my house is kind of shabby now. But we really are going to fix it up with paint and stuff. It won't ever be a mansion, but—"

"Who cares where you live!" Stephanie interrupted. "We just like *you*."

"Really?" Anna asked.

"Sure. We all acted pretty dumb," Stephanie told her. "Let's just call it even and forget it ever happened."

"Sounds good to me!" Anna said. "So, quick— tell me everything that's been happening since I've been gone."

"I have a better idea," Stephanie told her. "Come back to camp, and we'll have more time to tell you."

"I'm on my way!" Anna said.

"Great! I'll tell the others, and we'll see you soon!" Stephanie hung up the phone and cheered. *Hooray! I finally did something right! Darcy is back and Anna is back. Now all we need is for Cody to be the best swimming coach ever, and we've got it made!*

*   *   *

Rene strutted toward them, dripping wet from the pool. "I thought you might like to know that our new time is a *scorching* five minutes and fifty-two seconds." Rene held out the stopwatch so that Stephanie and her friends could see. "Read it and weep!"

"Why?" Stephanie asked. "Our new coach should be here later this afternoon. With his help, we'll beat your time."

Rene narrowed her eyes. "Who's your new coach?"

"That's for us to know—" Darcy started.

"And for you to worry about!" Stephanie added.

Stephanie and Darcy exchanged high fives. They turned their backs on Rene. Stephanie hadn't felt so happy in days. Things were definitely improving!

"I think you're going to win it, you guys," Anna told them. "I thought you looked terrific today."

"Thanks, Anna," Stephanie replied. "But we're not as fast as the Flamingoes. Not yet, anyway."

"Not until Cody gets here and gives us some winning tips," Kayla said.

Anna glanced at her watch. "Well, it was fun watching you swim. But I'm heading home now."

"No problem," Stephanie told her. "We'll see you back here tomorrow, at the picnic. Right?"

"You couldn't keep me away!" Anna replied. "Good luck, you guys!" She gave them all a big hug, then hurried off.

"I'm so glad we're all back together again," Allie said, grinning at Darcy. "It wouldn't be Club Stephanie without you and Anna."

"The five of us are a great team," Stephanie agreed.

"And a tired team," Darcy added. "Let's get drinks in the snack shack and take a long break. We want to be fresh for Cody."

"Good idea," Stephanie agreed.

As they finished their drinks at the snack shack, they talked about ways to improve their swim time.

"Hey, Kayla!"

Stephanie glanced up. A tall, good-looking guy waved and hurried toward their table. He had wavy brown hair and a deep tan.

"Here's Cody—right on time!" Kayla waved her arms in the air. "Hey, Cody!"

Kayla introduced him to Stephanie, Darcy, and Allie. Cody smiled, revealing two deep dimples. "When do we start?" he asked.

"Right away! We are so glad you're here," Kayla said. She glanced over her shoulder and leaned closer to Cody. "The girls I told you about—the

Flamingoes—finished their practice relay in record time today. We have to beat them, Cody. They've been making our lives miserable."

"Plus if we lose our race tomorrow, we'll have to wear shower caps to the pool for a day!" Stephanie added.

Cody laughed. "That sounds serious," he said. He pulled his stopwatch and a clipboard from his backpack. "I don't have time to change your strokes or anything. But if we concentrate on flip turns, I think I can really help."

"Okay!" Stephanie bounced to her feet. She felt more energetic than she had in days.

They hurried out of the snack shack and around the clubhouse. "There's the pool," Stephanie told Cody. "We usually—"

She came to a dead stop. "Oh, no!" she exclaimed. She stared at a sign propped up against the lifeguard's chair: POOL CLOSED DUE TO OVER-CHLORINATION.

"Bummer," Cody said. "I hate when they put fresh chlorine in the water! It takes forever for the smell to go away."

Stephanie, Darcy, Kayla, and Allie exchanged horrified looks.

"But—how could the pool be closed now?" Allie asked. "It's our last afternoon left to practice!"

"This is totally unfair!" Darcy exclaimed.

"It's worse than unfair," Kayla added. "It's a disaster! Now we can't practice with Cody. Which means—"

"That we're doomed," Stephanie finished. "We're going to lose the race for sure!"

CHAPTER
14

"I feel terrible," Darcy said. "Our last chance to get better—totally shot."

"You can't find another pool to use?" Cody asked.

"There *is* no other pool," Kayla replied.

No one said anything for a while.

"Hey, we tried," Kayla finally said.

"Come on, you guys, this isn't like us." Stephanie forced herself to sound cheerful. "We'll go out there tomorrow and swim our best, right? And in the meantime . . ."

Allie, Darcy, and Kayla stared at her. "In the meantime, what?" Allie asked.

"Let's do what we usually do when we're down. Go for pizza!"

An hour later, they finished their last slices.

"Well, that was an awesome pizza," Cody said. "I'm almost glad that your practice was canceled."

"Don't even joke about it," Stephanie told him.

Cody, Stephanie, and her friends were squeezed into a booth at Tony's Pizzeria. Tony's was *the* hangout for local kids. They had finished off one of Tony's giant super-special pizzas, and they'd been talking for what seemed like hours.

"It's nobody's fault that the pool was closed," Kayla said. "I just can't believe our bad luck."

Cody got a funny look on his face. "Don't look now, but these two girls just walked in, and they're dressed exactly alike. Pink *everything.*"

Stephanie glanced over her shoulder. *Yuck,* she thought, quickly turning back toward the table. Cynthia Hanson and Darah Judson were standing at the counter.

"Those girls are Flamingoes," Kayla explained to Cody in a low voice. "They're friends of the team we want to beat."

"They always wear something pink," Allie explained. "To look like flamingoes, I guess."

"That's dumb." Cody rattled the ice cubes in his cup and drained it. "I'm going to call my dad for a ride home. Anyone want anything else?" The girls all shook their heads. Cody climbed out of the booth and headed for the telephone.

"I feel awful that we dragged Cody to the pool for no reason," Allie told Kayla.

Kayla shrugged. "It's not a complete waste. I talked him into coming to the picnic tomorrow. He's totally psyched."

"What are you doing with such a cute guy?" a voice interrupted. "And who is he, anyway?"

Stephanie glanced up in surprise. Cynthia and Darah stood beside their booth.

"No one you'd be interested in," Stephanie told them. "He hates the color pink."

"Ha, ha," Cynthia said. "Really, who is he? I never saw him around before."

"He's my cousin, and he doesn't live around here," Kayla said. "Okay? And he won't be hanging around the pool, either," she added.

"Why not?" Darah asked.

"Because he only came today to coach our last practice," Darcy told them.

Darah and Cynthia exchanged amused looks. Darah giggled. "Yeah, your practice. Too bad it was canceled," she said.

"But you know how it is—when all that *chlorine* gets in your eyes," Cynthia added. She began to laugh, and Darah joined in as if they'd made a hilarious joke.

"It's just too easy to trick some people," Darah said. "You know that old saying, 'Don't believe everything you read'?" She snickered. "Well, sometimes reading is a *sign* of a stupid person."

Cynthia cracked up all over again. "I can't believe you all fell for that trick! You are so dense!"

"Right. Good luck at the race tomorrow— losers!" Darah and Cynthia hurried out of Tony's.

Cody slipped back into the booth. "What was that all about?" he asked.

"I can't believe it!" Stephanie felt ready to explode. "They did it again! The pool isn't full of chlorine!" she burst out. "The sign was a fake! A trick by the Flamingoes to make us miss our last practice!"

"You're kidding," Cody said. "They would do something that mean just to win one race?"

"Believe it," Kayla told him. "That's what we're up against."

"Wow." Cody shook his head in disbelief. "But it's sort of good news, too. I mean, if the pool is okay, we can head back there and practice after all."

Darcy glanced at her watch and groaned. "No, we can't. The pool closed five minutes ago."

110

"No wonder Cynthia and Darah told us the truth," Kayla said. "They knew it was too late for us to do anything about it."

Allie dropped her head into her hands. "Those Flamingoes are the worst! And now they're going to win tomorrow."

"Maybe not," Stephanie said. "I have an idea."

"Chain link." Cody shook the fence. "We can climb this, no problem."

Stephanie stared at the fence surrounding the community center. The whole place was officially closed. The pool was deserted. Only a few outside lights were on. It felt spooky to be the only ones there.

"Who's first?" Cody asked.

"I don't know." Allie hesitated. "I'm sort of afraid of heights. And that's about an eight-foot fence."

"Come *on*," Stephanie urged her. "We'll all help you."

"But what if we get caught?" Allie sounded super-nervous.

Stephanie was also nervous about getting caught. *If Dad finds out about this, he'll ground me for a week! No, a year*, she decided. But she wasn't about to let Allie know how she really felt.

"We've got to do it," Stephanie told her. "I'll go first."

Stephanie grabbed hold of the fence and climbed. She swung herself over the top, climbed down a couple of feet, and then dropped to the ground.

"Totally easy!" Stephanie said quietly. "You're next, Allie."

Cody gave Allie a boost up. Allie clung to the fence and then climbed slowly. "I hate this," she grumbled. But she reached the top, swung over, and dropped to the ground.

"Made it!" she exclaimed in a whisper.

Stephanie gave Allie a quick hug. "Good job," she said.

Darcy was already halfway over, and Kayla and Cody were right behind her. They hit the ground moments later.

"Okay, let's get to work," Cody told them. "But we have to be quiet."

An hour later, Allie performed a perfect flip turn and churned powerfully back down her lane. Kayla dove and hit the water at the same moment that Allie tagged the pool wall.

"That's it!" Cody whispered in excitement.

Kayla did a super-tight flip turn, then sped into her final lap. Cody's stopwatch clicked as she tagged the wall.

Stephanie peered over Cody's shoulder. "Well? How was our time?"

"Five minutes, forty-eight seconds," Cody reported.

Stephanie and Darcy exchanged shocked looks. "Say that again," Darcy demanded.

"Five, forty-eight," Cody said. "Why? Isn't that good enough?"

"No, it's *not* good!" Stephanie broke into an enormous grin. "It's *fantastic!* That's four seconds faster than the Flamingoes' best-ever time!"

"Cody, you're a genius!" Darcy exclaimed. "You knocked thirty seconds off our time!"

"That felt *so* good," Allie told him. "I did everything you said, Cody. I curled up really tight, and I nailed my flip turn."

"I noticed," Cody told her, grinning.

Kayla pulled herself out of the water. "Cody, you're an incredible coach. I tucked my head like you told me to, and I could feel that my body was straighter in the water and my legs had tons more kick. It was amazing!"

"Our time was amazing, too," Stephanie told Kayla. "We might actually win tomorrow!"

"What did I tell you?" Kayla beamed with pride. "My cousin is about the best coach in the history of the world."

Stephanie was so excited that she forgot to be quiet. "We're going to win!" she exclaimed.

"We're going to win! We're going to win!" the others chanted. "We're going to—"

"Exactly what are you kids doing?" a voice demanded.

Stephanie spun around. "Oh, no!" she cried.

CHAPTER
15

◆ ◢ ◆ ◆

"Sandy—what are you doing here?" Stephanie stared at her in horror.

"Getting ready for tomorrow," Sandy said. "But the real question is, What are *you* doing here?"

"I can explain that," Stephanie said.

If you give me about two years to think of a good excuse, she added to herself.

"I'm waiting." Sandy tapped her foot impatiently.

Stephanie shot Darcy a look that meant *help!*

"We had to practice for the race tomorrow," Darcy blurted.

Sandy stared at Darcy as if she were crazy. "What's wrong with practicing when the pool is open?"

"We tried!" Stephanie exclaimed. "But we thought the pool was closed when Rene and the . . . oops." Stephanie hadn't meant to tell on Rene. But it was too late to take it back now.

"What about Rene?" Sandy prodded.

"Well, *somebody* put up a sign saying that the pool was overchlorinated," Allie rushed to explain.

"I was here till the pool closed today," Sandy told them. "I didn't see any sign like that."

"They must have taken it down after we left," Stephanie said.

Sandy looked closely at Stephanie, then at Darcy, Kayla, and Allie. She took a deep breath and let it out all at once. "I guess I believe you. I trust you, or I wouldn't have let you run Club Stephanie. But I'm sure you girls know that sneaking in here after hours is completely unacceptable."

"We know," Stephanie answered.

"And climbing in over the fence . . ." Sandy paused. "If something happened to any of you, the pool could have been sued. Maybe even shut down."

"We're really sorry," Kayla said in a small voice.

Stephanie nodded. "It was a stupid thing to do."

"And we'll never do it again," Darcy added.

"You'd better not!" Sandy frowned. "Not that you'd *want* to—not after you get through with your punishment."

"Punishment?" Stephanie felt a burst of alarm. "You're not going to kick us out of the pool, are you?"

"You will let us swim in the race tomorrow, won't you?" Darcy added.

Sandy looked thoughtful. "I don't want to spoil the picnic tomorrow. So I'll let you swim."

"Yes!" Stephanie and the others cheered. Stephanie had never felt so relieved in her life.

"Don't celebrate yet," Sandy warned. "You'll start your punishment the day *after* tomorrow. And it will be a good one. There's an awful lot of work to do around this place. Like painting and cleaning and all kinds of odd jobs. I'm sure I'll think of enough chores to keep you busy for the rest of the summer."

"No problem," Stephanie told her. "Working hard will be easy for a bunch of winners like us!"

"Wow!"" Michelle stared as the Tanner family filed through the turnstile. "I've never seen this place so crowded!"

"Or so beautiful!" Stephanie added.

Bright red, white, and blue flags fluttered everywhere in the community center. An arch of red, white, and blue balloons towered over the pool entrance. Hundreds of tiny American flags fluttered from the fence. Streamers crisscrossed the roof of the clubhouse and ran out to the snack shack and over the open patio. Lanterns swung in the breeze.

The Fourth of July had never looked so festive!

Crowds of people pushed everywhere. The air was filled with excitement. Stephanie could already smell hot dogs and hamburgers cooking on a dozen different grills.

"Let's grab a picnic spot on the field," Danny suggested. "It's filling up fast."

"Fine with me!" D.J. agreed. She nearly staggered under the weight of the picnic basket she was holding with Zach, her date for the day.

"I see a good spot." Stephanie pointed to a patch of lawn under one of the shade trees.

Uncle Jesse lifted Nicky down from his shoulders and set him on the ground. "Go save that spot!" he ordered. Nicky and Alex both took off running. "Wait, don't forget me," Jesse cried. He chased after them.

Joey fell into step beside Stephanie. "So when do your peewee races begin? I want to watch the three-legged race."

"Joey, you probably want to *be* in the three-legged race," Stephanie teased. "They're on the playing fields in an hour. But the peewee swim race is—yikes! In three minutes!" Stephanie set down her thermos and took off for the pool.

Darcy and Kayla were lining up the kids for their first race. Allie waited with Anna at the finish line, holding bags full of prizes.

"Did I miss anything?" Stephanie asked Allie.

"Nope," she said. "The first race is about to start."

The peewee races went by in a blur. Austin was thrilled when he won a giant balloon for holding his breath underwater.

Tyler won for scooping up the most water rings. All the kids won some kind of a prize—but mostly they had fun.

Then it was time for the field races. Stephanie and the others gave away piles of candy and toys and more balloons. Finally Anna helped the Club Stephanie campers line up to get ready for their parade.

"The Star-Spangled Banner" blared over the loudspeakers.

"We're on," Anna called. She led the Club Stephanie kids down the clubhouse stairs and across the playing fields. Each kid proudly carried a flag.

"They're so cute!" Allie exclaimed.

Stephanie nodded happily. Each camper's flag was unique. Austin's had a picture of a super-hero with a cape flying behind him. Tyler's had an adorable tiger.

The crowd laughed and applauded. The kids

were beaming as they finished their parade back at the snack shack, where cold drinks were waiting for them.

Stephanie, Allie, Kayla, and Darcy hurried over and gave Anna a thumbs-up. "Your flags were a total success!" Stephanie exclaimed.

"Thanks!" Anna beamed with pride.

"But now it's almost time for our race," Allie announced. "Is anybody else as nervous as I am?" She chewed her fingernails.

Stephanie threw her arms around Allie. "Nervous—who, me? I can't wait to beat the tans off those Flamingoes! Let's go suit up."

Stephanie led Allie, Darcy, and Kayla into the locker room. They quickly changed into their racing suits and headed back to the pool. Stephanie saw Rick huddled with the Flamingoes, giving them last-minute tips before their race.

I don't care, she told herself. *I won't let any of them bother me—not now!*

Stephanie turned to Kayla. "Where's Cody?" she asked. "He said he might have some last-minute tips for us."

"There," Kayla replied in a weak voice. She hunched over, holding her stomach, and pointed ahead. Cody and Anna were waiting for them at the shallow end of the pool.

Stephanie peered at Kayla's face. "Hey—are you okay? You look awfully pale."

"I don't feel so great," Kayla answered. "Cody said my uncle Dan has the flu. And—" She suddenly covered her mouth with her hand. "Oh, no! I'm going to be sick!" She staggered back toward the clubhouse. Cody and Anna saw her leave and rushed over to Stephanie.

"What happened? What's wrong with Kayla?" Anna asked.

"She's sick!" Stephanie exclaimed. "I don't believe this!"

At that moment, Sandy blew her whistle. "We're ready for the girls medley relay races. Flamingoes versus Club Stephanie. Swimmers, please line up!"

Darcy shot Stephanie a horrified look. "What are we going to do now?" she asked. "Kayla is too sick to swim, and we need to have four people on our team."

"Can't one of us swim two turns?" Allie asked.

"You know you can't," Cody told her. "It's not allowed. This is strictly a four-person relay."

Stephanie swallowed hard. "We don't have any choice," she said. "We have to drop out of the race!"

CHAPTER
16

◆ ◂ ◾ ◆

"I'm sorry, but you're right. You have to drop out," Sandy said. Stephanie, Allie, and Darcy groaned together.

"I'm so sorry, you guys," Anna told them.

"What's going on?" Rene demanded, pushing her way up to them. "What's this about dropping out?"

The other Flamingoes gathered around her.

"What's the matter? Are you scared to lose in public?" Tiffany jeered. The other Flamingoes snickered.

"We're not scared," Stephanie told her. "We have a big problem. Kayla's sick. She can't swim."

"What if we get someone to replace Kayla?"

Darcy asked Sandy. "That would be okay, wouldn't it? I mean, we all worked so hard to get ready for this race."

"Would that be okay?" Stephanie added.

"Sure, that would be fine." Sandy smiled kindly at them. "But who could fill in at the last moment?"

"Anna! She could do it!" Stephanie exclaimed.

Anna stared at her in disbelief. "Me?"

Allie and Darcy exchanged a look of surprise.

Anna cleared her throat. "Uh, Stephanie, thanks for thinking I could do it. But I haven't touched the water once this summer!"

"Listen, we know you're not a great swimmer," Stephanie admitted. "But all you have to do is stay afloat for two laps. You can swim any way you can. You can doggie-paddle if you have to."

"I don't know. . . ." Anna hesitated.

"We can't even try without you. Please?" Stephanie begged.

Darcy, Allie, and Stephanie looked at her.

"You're on," Anna finally said. "I'll take Kayla's place."

"Great," Sandy said. "I'll give you a few minutes to get ready. Then we'll have the backstrokers in the water."

"All right!" Stephanie cheered. "Let's do it!"

Stephanie and Darcy led Anna to the locker room.

"You're about my size," Darcy said. She pulled her spare black racing suit from her locker and handed it to Anna.

"Okay. I just hope you guys won't be too disappointed in me," Anna said.

"Anna, you're saving our lives. We couldn't be disappointed," Stephanie assured her.

Anna dressed quickly while Darcy and Stephanie gave her as many pointers as they could think of.

"Ready," Anna announced. She took a deep breath. "I'm not sure I'll remember any of the stuff you're telling me," she admitted. "But I'll do my best."

"That's all we want," Stephanie told her.

Back at the pool, Stephanie saw the Flamingoes give Anna a curious look. Stephanie didn't blame them. After all, Anna hadn't been in the water once all summer.

Stephanie leaped into the water, taking Kayla's place for the backstroke.

"Way to go, Steph!" she heard her family cheering. But she didn't have time to look their way. Julie Chu was already in position in the next lane.

Please, please, let us do our best, Stephanie thought.

"Ready, swimmers?" Sandy called.

Stephanie and Julie nodded.

"On your mark!" Sandy bellowed. "Go!"

Stephanie and Julie threw themselves backward into the water. Stephanie worked harder than ever before. She tried to remember everything she knew about swimming a strong, fast backstroke. She finished a half lap ahead of Julie. Awesome!

Then it was Anna's turn. She plunged awkwardly into the water and began to do a choppy crawl. Stephanie climbed out of the pool as Alyssa dove in for the Flamingoes.

Don't let Anna stop, she thought. *Whatever happens, let her make it two full laps!*

She was almost afraid to watch, but she made herself look. Anna moved slowly but steadily toward the far end of the pool. She had changed to a sidestroke as Alyssa began her return lap.

"Come on, Anna!" Allie and Darcy were screaming.

"Okay, get ready." Cody nodded to Darcy. "Your butterfly is next. And we need you to make up some serious time."

"No problem." Darcy looked totally focused. She waited in diving position.

Rene was already in position to swim the third leg of the race. Alyssa drew close to the wall. Rene dove. Alyssa tagged the wall.

"Wait" Stephanie screamed. "Rene jumped her start!"

Tweeeeet!

Sandy's whistle rang out shrilly across the pool.

"Flamingoes—start over!" Sandy commanded.

"Yes!" Stephanie and Darcy slapped a high five. Rene turned around and swam back to the wall. She climbed back out of the pool. Sandy nodded and Rene dove again.

Anna finished her lap and tagged the wall. Stephanie and Darcy cheered.

"Go, Darcy!" Cody commanded. Darcy dove.

"This is great," Cody told Stephanie and the others. "It's just the break we needed! Rene just lost tons of time. Unless the others make it up, we could really win!"

Stephanie stared at Rene as she streaked through the water.

Only one leg left to go, Stephanie thought.

Cody reached a hand down to Anna. "Great job," he told her.

"You were fantastic!" Stephanie added. "We're only one length behind. We can win, Anna! We can win!"

"Great," Anna managed to say between breaths. She hung on to Cody's hand as she climbed out of the pool. Stephanie and Allie gave her a quick hug, then turned to cheer Darcy on.

"Go, Darcy!" they all yelled together. The crowd lined up around the pool. Everyone was going wild as Darcy swam incredibly fast.

Darcy pulled an entire body length closer to Rene.

Stephanie felt more nervous than she'd ever felt in her life. "Go, Darcy!" she screamed. "You can do it!"

A few feet away, the Flamingoes were shouting, "Go, Rene!"

Darcy reached the end of the pool and did the sleekest flip turn ever. Seconds later, she was speeding through her return lap. But Rene was still ahead.

"Go, go, go!" Stephanie screamed.

Darcy pulled even to Rene. She put on a final burst of speed and tagged the wall first.

Allie dove in. She pulled down the lane with strong, deep strokes. She didn't lose a minute of Darcy's lead time. Mary dove for the Flamingoes as Allie neared the far wall of the pool.

"Keep it tight, Allie!" Stephanie screamed. Darcy and Anna were screaming and jumping up and down. Cody was cheering and pumping his fist in the air.

"Go, Allie! Go!" Cody yelled. "You have her beat by a mile!"

Allie did the tightest flip turn Stephanie had ever

seen. A second later, she was streaking through her final lap.

"You can do it!" Stephanie screamed. "Go! Go! Go!"

Allie tagged the wall to win the race.

"She won! We did it! Club Stephanie rules!" Stephanie, Darcy, and Anna went crazy, jumping up and down and screaming at the top of their lungs. Even Cody started jumping.

Allie pulled herself out of the water. She pushed up her goggles, threw her arms around Stephanie, and started screaming, too.

"We did it!" Darcy kept saying. "We did it!"

"Hey—check out the Flamingoes," Cody told them.

Stephanie glanced at Rene and her friends. "You call that a flip turn?" Rene screeched at Mary as Mary finished her final lap.

"Don't talk about *me!* What about *your* false start? You lost the race for us!" Mary fumed.

"Those Flamingoes better not fight," Stephanie told Darcy. "They'll need all the friends they can get next week."

"Right," Darcy added. "After all, who else will talk to a bunch of girls wearing shower caps?" She and Stephanie giggled.

"Stephanie! Over here!"

Stephanie looked up to find her dad's video camera pointed straight at her. She nudged Darcy and grinned. All of Club Stephanie—including Cody—smiled and waved at the camera.

"The winners!" Cody announced. He slapped high fives with each of them.

Stephanie beamed. It felt great to be a winner! She turned to find Sandy—and saw Rick staring right at her.

Talk to me. Say anything! Stephanie silently begged. *Please, let me know you don't hate me!*

But Rick dropped his eyes. He turned and disappeared into the crowd.

Suddenly Stephanie didn't feel so terrific anymore.

CHAPTER
17

◆ ◀ ▸ ◆

"What a day!" said Anna. "Our campers had the most fun ever, we won our race, and the fireworks will be starting soon. What more could anyone want?"

I want Rick to like me again, that's what! Stephanie silently answered.

The awful part was, Rick wasn't the least bit interested in her anymore. He couldn't have made it any clearer.

Stephanie sighed and stretched out on the red-and-white picnic blanket. Allie gave her a smile.

"You don't seem too happy," Allie commented. "Considering all the great stuff that happened today."

"Of course I'm happy," Stephanie told her. She forced a giant smile.

"I'm so sorry Kayla had to go home," Darcy said.

"I feel bad for her," Stephanie agreed. "She's missing a really fun time."

Cody smiled at her. "Yeah. I'm having a *great* time." He wiped his hands with a napkin. "Anyone want more fried chicken?" he asked. "Stephanie?"

"No, thanks," Stephanie said. "I don't have much appetite."

Cody moved over to help himself to more fried chicken from their picnic basket. He started talking to Anna.

Allie nudged Stephanie. "I think Cody has a crush on you, Steph," she whispered.

"What?" Stephanie blinked in surprise. "You're kidding, right?" she whispered back.

"No, I think he really likes you," Allie replied. "So, are you interested?"

"I don't know. I have to think about it," Stephanie said. She frowned.

Cody was really nice, and cute and talented. There was no reason *not* to like him—except for the fact that he wasn't Rick.

Stephanie shook her head. "I'm not ready to like any boy yet," she told Allie.

"You aren't over Rick, huh?" Allie gave her a sympathetic look.

"Guess not," Stephanie said.

Cody moved back on the blanket until he was sitting next to Stephanie again. "Your dad is one great cook," he told her.

"Yeah, he's pretty good," Stephanie replied.

"Uh-oh. Flamingo alert," Darcy warned.

Stephanie looked up. Rene, Alyssa, and Mary strolled by—and Rick was with them! He walked close by Rene's side. As they came close to Stephanie's blanket, Rene draped her arm around Rick's shoulders. She looked straight into his eyes and laughed at something he said. Stephanie felt a burst of anger.

"I love this chicken!" Cody declared, taking another bite.

"Oh, Cody, you're so funny!" Stephanie exclaimed. She laughed even louder than Rene and slipped *her* arm around Cody's shoulders. Cody looked at her in surprise.

Stephanie watched Rick. For an instant, he seemed angry. Then he smiled and wrapped his arm around Rene's waist. Rene smiled happily up at him. They headed toward the Flamingoes' pink blanket.

That's it! That's the last time I let Rick get to me, Stephanie ordered herself.

Then she realized she still had her arm around Cody's shoulders. Her face flushed, and she snatched her arm away. Cody stared at her, and there was an awkward silence.

"I, uh—thanks again for helping us win today, Cody," she said.

"Oh. You're welcome." Cody cleared his throat and moved closer to her. "Uh, you and your friends are great. I really like all of you. But—"

Boom!

A burst of bright red and white sparkles lit the sky overhead.

"Oh! Look! The fireworks are starting!" Stephanie exclaimed. She jumped up. "I've got to get some pictures of this!"

She pulled her camera out of her backpack and ran away before Cody could say another word. She didn't stop until she was far away from her blanket.

"Stephanie!"

Stephanie spun around. "Rick!" She stumbled backward in confusion and stared at him. It was too dark to read his expression clearly.

"W-What do you want?" she stammered. "Where's Rene?" Her voice came out colder than she meant it to.

Rick's lips drew together in a tight line. "I'm not

stuck to Rene, you know," he replied. "And I don't *want* anything from you! I was going to tell you— I thought we could talk, and—" He broke off. "Never mind," he snapped. "It was stupid, I guess."

Stephanie swallowed hard. "Well, then I guess we still have nothing to say to each other."

Please, please don't go, she thought, staring at him.

A muscle in Rick's jaw was twitching. "That's okay with me," he responded.

Boom! Boom!

More fireworks exploded overhead. Stephanie turned her head in time to see a wild burst of gold and white lights. When she turned back, Rick was pulling something out of his pocket.

"In fact, I'd be happy if you never spoke to me again," he was saying. "Or *wrote* to me, either!"

He shoved a crumpled piece of paper at her. She reached automatically to take it from him. She stared stupidly down at his hand. A ball of writing paper.

Stephanie gasped.

My letter!

Stephanie stared down at it. For an instant, she remembered how happy she felt when she wrote it. And how miserable she was now.

A tiny cry escaped her throat. She blinked hard to keep back the tears that flooded her eyes.

Boom! Boom!

The ground beneath her feet turned yellow, then blue in the reflected light. She smoothed the crumpled paper on her knee.

A brilliant white blast of light turned the night as bright as day. The black ink stood out sharply against the white paper.

Wait! I wrote my letter in purple ink, Stephanie thought. *Definitely! I used Allie's special purple pen— on purple paper!*

Stephanie ran over to a hanging lantern. She lifted the paper into the light.

It wasn't her letter! This was a short note, written in loopy, scrawling handwriting.

As she read it, her eyes grew wide in horror:

Dear Rick:

I'm breaking up with you, because you're a terrible kisser.

Sorry, Stephanie

Stephanie thought back to the day she'd left Rick the note. She remembered tucking the purple envelope into Rick's backpack. She remembered talking to Alyssa after Rick had gone home sick. She remembered finding the opened envelope.

But who had taken the envelope from Rick's

backpack? Who had opened it? Rick—or someone else?

A chill ran down Stephanie's spine.

What if Rick never even saw the letter she wrote? What if the Flamingoes had stolen it first!

That's it, she realized. *That's exactly what happened!*

Someone—Alyssa or another Flamingo—had slipped her letter from the envelope. They had written their own message and given Rick this horrible note instead.

Rick had no idea she tried to make up with him. He had no idea how much she still liked him!

No wonder Rick wouldn't look at me or speak to me after he read this. Who would? she thought.

It was the most humiliating, embarrassing note any boy could ever receive.

"Steph! Steph—where are you?" Allie spotted Stephanie under the lantern light and ran panting up to her side. "Stephanie, what are you doing alone over here? What's going on?"

"I just found out why Rick's been acting so weird," Stephanie told her. "It's all because of the Flamingoes! But this time they've gone too far," she declared. "And they're not going to get away with it."

Stephanie angrily crumpled the note in her fist. "I've got to find Rick and tell him the whole truth about the Flamingoes," she said. "And then it's time for revenge!"

Rene and the Flamingoes have finally gone too far. It's payback time! What will Stephanie and her friends do to get even? Read FULL HOUSE/ CLUB STEPHANIE #3, *Flamingo Revenge*, to find out!

FULL HOUSE™
Stephanie

PHONE CALL FROM A FLAMINGO	88004-7/$3.99
THE BOY-OH-BOY NEXT DOOR	88121-3/$3.99
TWIN TROUBLES	88290-2/$3.99
HIP HOP TILL YOU DROP	88291-0/$3.99
HERE COMES THE BRAND NEW ME	89858-2/$3.99
THE SECRET'S OUT	89859-0/$3.99
DADDY'S NOT-SO-LITTLE GIRL	89860-4/$3.99
P.S. FRIENDS FOREVER	89861-2/$3.99
GETTING EVEN WITH THE FLAMINGOES	52273-6/$3.99
THE DUDE OF MY DREAMS	52274-4/$3.99
BACK-TO-SCHOOL COOL	52275-2/$3.99
PICTURE ME FAMOUS	52276-0/$3.99
TWO-FOR-ONE CHRISTMAS FUN	53546-3/$3.99
THE BIG FIX-UP MIX-UP	53547-1/$3.99
TEN WAYS TO WRECK A DATE	53548-X/$3.99
WISH UPON A VCR	53549-8/$3.99
DOUBLES OR NOTHING	56841-8/$3.99
SUGAR AND SPICE ADVICE	56842-6/$3.99
NEVER TRUST A FLAMINGO	56843-4/$3.99
THE TRUTH ABOUT BOYS	00361-5/$3.99
CRAZY ABOUT THE FUTURE	00362-3/$3.99